SORCERESS ETERNAL

LISA BLACKWOOD

SORCERESS ETERNAL

A Gargoyle and Sorceress Tale / Book 9

Lisa Blackwood

Sorceress Eternal

Gargoyle & Sorceress Book 9

Sorceress Eternal © 2019 by Lisa Smeaton

http://lisablackwood.com/

COVER DESIGNED BY: Heather Hamilton-Senter

PRINT ISBN: 978-1-990608-55-1

EDITION: 10/27/2021

❀ Created with Vellum

BOOKS BY LISA BLACKWOOD

Gargoyle & Sorceress

Dawn of the Sorceress

Sorceress Awakening

Sorceress Rising

Sorceress Hunting

Sorceress at War

Sorceress Enraged

Legacy of the Sorceress

Sorcery & Firedrakes

Scion of the Sorceress

Sorceress Eternal

In Deception's Shadow Series (Epic Fantasy Romance)

Betrayal's Price

Herd Mistress

Maiden's Wolf

Death's Queen

The Prince's Gryphon (forthcoming)

Ishtar's Legacy Series (Epic Fantasy Romance)

Ishtar's Blade

The Blade's Beginning (short story)

Blade's Honor

Blade's Destiny

The Blade's Shadow

First Queen of the Gryphons

The King of the Anunnaki (forthcoming)

The Anunnaki's Blade (forthcoming)

Huntress vs Huntsman (Epic Fantasy Romance)

Master of the Hunt

Night Huntress

Dragon Archer

Soul Mage (forthcoming)

Sorceress Eternal

Don't miss the stunning conclusion to the epic Gargoyle & Sorceress tales.

The final battle between the servants of the Divine Ones and the Battle Goddess's twisted ambition has arrived.

All three Realms are in peril and Earth might be the first to fall. But Lillian, Gregory, and their allies will not allow so many innocents to pay the price for a demigoddess's insanity. This time, the Lady of Battle may have set in motion her own doom.

Yet, in battle, the outcome is never certain, and the Avatars might yet have to pay the debt so rarely paid.

SORCERESS ETERNAL

CHAPTER ONE

Erika

The ancient Chinese curse 'may you live in interesting times' which wasn't, in fact, ancient or Chinese in origin was still a perfect curse for Erika's present situation. Because life couldn't get much more interesting than having one four-armed and four-legged titan scoop you up and gallop away as another even older demigod gave chase. And they, in turn, were both being hunted by a really pissed off fire elemental.

Interesting times indeed.

The normal skin-tingling sensation of her gift feeding had revved up far past a mild tingling and was now a burning itch between muscles and overlying skin.

And that wasn't even the worst of it. With each of the titan's strides, the shock of his hooves striking the ground traveled up his frame and into her body until she was bouncing up and down in the cage of his fingers. For the first time in her life, she could relate to a rubber ball in an energetic child's hands.

At last, the creature everyone called Lord Death slowed. After a moment, she realized she could hear the sound of the ocean over the rushing of blood in her head. Then there came one final round of bouncing before all motion ceased. She'd ridden enough horses to know the demigod had just skidded to a hasty halt likely because something unexpected blocked his path.

Light appeared between his fingers as one of the hands holding her trapped lifted away. She blinked against the sudden brightness but was soon able to see a gargoyle hovering in the air directly in the demigod's path. Beyond the gargoyle's shoulder, tall ocean waves rolled into shore.

It would have been pretty if she hadn't also suspected the demigod holding her planned to gallop straight into the ocean and hold her below the surface. Even as her gift continued to suck the magic from the demigod, she knew she'd never be able to drain him fast enough to stop him from galloping into the ocean with her.

Briefly, she flashed back to the time when she'd faced the assassin spell, and Gryton had told her it was too risky to attack, that she might not be ready to face such a foe. He'd later told her she would need much more practice before facing off against the Lord of the Underworld.

Seemed Hot Stuff was right.

"Release the Null, Draydrak," Gregory barked out the order. "My Sorceress tells me you have already succeeded in what you really planned."

"It is as the Divine Ones said," Draydrak agreed.

"Are you going to release the Null? Or must I take her from you?"

The Lord of the Underworld snorted. "I have no wish to fight you. I know I won't win. However, there is one more thing Gryton needs to realize to finish his maturation."

Erika scowled in sudden understanding. This wasn't about her powers as a Null. This was entirely about Gryton.

She was bait.

Unfortunately for Lord Draydrak, no one had told him she was no helpless, whimpering female in need of rescuing. And now that they were on a sandy beach to judge by the sound of the titan's footfalls, a fall to the ground likely wouldn't break anything.

Dropping to her hands and knees, she pressed her hands against the skin of the giant's palm.

While she might not be able to absorb enough power to incapacitate Lord Death, she should be able to drain him enough to allow the Avatar an easier win. And if she managed to paralyze his hand? That was one less to hold a sword.

As her gift continued to feed, the burning pain under her skin edged up a notch. She looked up at Gregory, hoping for a distraction to take her mind off the pain.

She wasn't disappointed.

Where Gregory had been hovering only a moment ago, now a pulsing ball of light was expanding out in some kind of spell. It grew taller by the second, shifting and flowing with purpose until it was twice as tall as the mountainous demigod.

Lord Draydrak drew three of his swords, his fourth remaining in its sheath since he couldn't put her down. Or perhaps his hand was paralyzed by her feeding as she'd hoped. Whatever the reason, Lord Death advanced upon the Avatar with only three of his four swords drawn.

Which might be more than enough since, as far as she could tell, Gregory wasn't wielding a weapon. Though perhaps the shimmering ropes of power expanding outward *were* becoming weapons.

Lord Death burst into motion once more, forcing Erika to grab at his large fingers or risk rolling off his palm, and by the sound of his hooves scrambling over loose rocks, the ground below was no longer going to be a soft landing if she fell. When she was able to look back up, it was to see the Avatar's magic had taken on a vaguely humanoid shape.

Draydrak reared back, leaping away from a wave of power directed at him. By the sound, he was once more on sandy beach.

The next moment, the demigod was leaning down to deposit her roughly on the shore as he continued to gallop down the beach. She only had a moment to register the warmth of the sand and the scent of the ocean before she forced herself up. An act that was made more difficult by her burning muscles. But she made it to her feet.

Draydrak was now a good two hundred feet down the beach. Gregory was much closer, crouched down with his wings folded around him. After rushing up to the gargoyle, she discovered she was standing next to a stone statue.

What on God's green earth?

She glanced back up at the towering magic she'd mistaken for the beginnings of a spell. But this was no spell. The bright magic swirling and snapping in the breeze was taking on shape and substance. She could now see wings, a tail, and other gargoyle features as she studied the glowing godlike being.

He burned with more power than she'd ever felt in her life. He reminded her of a sun. A living sun. One that was facing down Lord Death.

Erika blinked in shock as she fully realized what she was seeing.

The Avatar soul. Or at least one half of it.

She took several stumbling steps away from the two demigods, but her eyes slid back to the statue of what had once been a flesh and blood gargoyle. Hundreds of luminescent tendrils of magic trailed up from the statue to disappear into the shimmering core of the Avatar's soul.

He wasn't dead, then. At least, she didn't think he'd permanently abandoned his body.

But it did look like the two were readying to give each other a spectacular beatdown at any moment, and there wasn't one thing she could do to stop them. She moved farther down the beach, hoping to survive whatever was about to happen.

Just as she climbed the first dune, a roar split the air—and she swore she actually felt it in her feet. Stumbling, she fell forward onto the sand. When she looked up in the direction of the roar, she saw a massive dragon burning with molten power.

As the beast neared, her soul link flared wide, and she knew she was looking at Gryton.

He'd shifted to his dragon form. The one thing he'd said he'd never do.

"My Null!" The resounding thought was accompanied by another of his fierce, ground-shaking roars.

Draydrak and the Avatar soul turned to watch the dragon's approach.

The massive dragon was upon them in three wingbeats, his forelegs outstretched before him. He managed to snatch at both Draydrak and the Avatar. Then the dragon's momentum carried them all out into the waves.

Steam boiled up, obscuring Erika's view of the fight.

And it was a fight. There was no doubt in her mind that Gryton was trying to kill them. The dragon wasn't rational. There was no way he could defeat them both. Perhaps he could take down Draydrak on his own, but Erika had felt the Avatar's power.

But hadn't Gryton told her he'd lose everything he was, everything he'd worked for if he shifted to dragon form? Gryton was gone. This was the elemental dragon, and clearly it didn't think anything like the man.

And if Erika didn't do something, the Avatar might be forced to kill his own son. Was that Lord Death's plan all along? Despite the heat of the sun and the warm sand under her boots, a chill flowed across her soul.

She hadn't expected something so heartless from a servant of the so-called Light.

But could a creature that was death incarnate even have a heart, feel compassion, or experience remorse? Could such a being even perform his duty with such softness?

Erika was still formulating a plan when Anna and

Obsidian came in for a landing next to her. She glanced at them both and then back at Gryton.

"What the hell!" Anna shouted as she gawked at the demigod brawl.

"Indeed." Obsidian stepped in front of Anna as if instinctively trying to protect his Kyrsu.

Erika almost told him not to bother. If that ball of unbridled rage rolled back in their direction, they'd all get mowed down and incinerated. But there was another danger. "Gryton is losing cohesion. I can feel it. We need to find some way to separate him from the other two."

"I might have an idea about that," the Sorceress announced, as she joined them.

Erika glanced over her shoulder in time to see Lillian and Thayn come in for a landing next to them. For the first time since Lord Draydrak had snatched her up in his grasp, Erika felt hope.

"Lord Draydrak didn't actually want to harm you," the Sorceress explained. "He doesn't even want to harm my son. This was all an elaborate event put into motion by the Divine Ones."

Erika's stomach dropped. "They want Gryton dead?"

She was surprised by the strength of the fear gripping her at the thought of Gryton's death. Sure, he was a prickly asshole at times, but he wasn't all bad. And somehow, he'd wormed his way into her heart. She felt equal parts pity and compassion for him. As impossible as it would have seemed when she'd first met him, he was now her friend.

"No. The Divine Ones do not want him dead. They have a task for him to fulfill." The Sorceress's words were so different from what Erika had expected, her mind had trouble processing them.

"They don't want him dead? Why the hell did they set Lord Death upon him then?"

The Sorceress continued to call upon her own magic as she answered. "They didn't set Draydrak upon him. Not in the way you mean. They must know something that we do not, and they have deemed that it is time for Gryton to finally mature. His fear of his elemental dragon's chaotic nature has been holding him back for centuries. He must accept all sides of his nature if he has any hope of surviving the coming war and defeating the Battle Goddess. The Divine Ones knew he needed an incentive to overcome his reluctance to embrace his dragon side."

Erika's nostrils flared. "The Divine Ones needed bait."

"Yes. You were the incentive Gryton needed to overcome his own hesitation."

"Not possible. He hates me."

Lillian laughed at her. "You're wrong. You are the one being, besides myself, he has allowed himself to care for. When he thought Lord Draydrak was going to kill you, it brought his dragon nature to the surface."

Erika looked out at the brawl in the shallows. Steam and sea spray filled the air, forming a thick magic haze that was spreading in all directions.

A moment later, Lord Draydrak emerged from the magic fog, water streaming from his flanks as he rose out of the ocean. He heaved himself closer to shore, his mighty haunches powering him up the beach. But he only made it a short distance before a serpentine head emerged from the churning mess along the shoreline and snapped his jaws closed on one of Draydrak's hind legs.

The demigod snarled something in a foreign language and twisted, two of his swords slashing toward the dragon's neck. The dragon released the demigod and twisted out of reach before Lord Death could land a blow. Behind them, the Avatar rose up out of the water, towering over them both. If Erika wasn't misremembering, he was even bigger —and more pissed off looking—than he'd been the first time she'd seen him like this.

The dragon, sensing danger, attempted to bolt away from his father, but the Avatar snatched him up and tossed him farther down the beach. The dragon rolled, scrambling for footing. Digging in, he slowed himself and then came to a stop. Spinning toward his father, he opened his mouth wide and spewed fire.

The big demigod recoiled, suggesting his son's fire was damaging to one even as powerful as him.

But as illogical as it was, Erika was concerned for the dragon. Fire was now bleeding between his scales and dripping from his mouth. A river of it streamed from between the dragon's horns and flowed down his spine to the tip of his tail.

She didn't know how much more power the dragon could call upon without tipping over the edge and losing all control. If that happened, Gryton might die and take out a vast chunk of this world with him.

It was like the assassin spell all over again. Only here the opponents were too powerful for her to drain dry and neutralize.

Erika glanced back at Lord Draydrak, but he was just

standing there, waiting with his four swords at the ready. Perhaps she no longer had to worry about him.

She glanced toward the other titan in time to see the Avatar unfurling his massive gleaming wings, blocking out the horizon with their size. She thought he was going to take to the air and continue the attack, but as he beat his wings, he angled them in such a way as to fly backward with each beat as if he was a giant hummingbird.

When he touched down again, he was between them and the dragon.

"Our son is losing control, my Sorceress. I cannot force him to surrender," the titan acknowledged, growing concern and something like sadness entering his voice. "If the Null cannot calm him, you know what we must do for the good of all."

Erika attempted to stare a hole through the Sorceress. "What the hell is he talking about? He can't mean what I think he means. I won't let you kill Gryton."

Erika began to advance upon the Sorceress, her Null's ability stirring because of her fear.

Lillian gripped Erika's hands. "Easy. We won't kill him, but nor can we allow him to remain here and destroy this world. If we have to, I will create a portal spell to the Spirit Realm and with Lord Draydrak's help, my other half will force the dragon through."

"What will that do to Gryton?"

"I don't know if the one we know as Gryton will ever calm enough to resurface, but our son will live."

"That's a bullshit plan."

"Yes. And the Divine Ones never do something without

purpose. That is why I think they have something more in mind for you and G—"

A low rumble issued from the dragon. Erika tensed as the beast's head on its long serpentine neck darted low to the ground and then snaked from side to side until his gaze locked on her. In a flash, he was dashing across the damp sand.

Shit. For such a big creature, he was surprisingly fast on his feet.

The dragon roared a third time as he charged toward her location. Erika thought she might now know what the early mammals felt like when a rampaging saber-toothed predator ran at them.

The gargoyle titan slammed the dragon with his powerful tail, knocking him off his feet again. The beast didn't stay down more than a moment, and then he was back on his feet and lunging at his father. In swift retaliation, the dragon managed to slam his own tail into the Avatar. While his father was off balance, the dragon roared and breathed more fire upon the Avatar.

Beside Erika, the Sorceress hissed as if in pain herself. She must be feeling the damage to her other half. But before the dragon could inflict another blow, Lord Draydrak galloped back into the battle, driving both opponents toward the group gathered around Erika.

"Fuck this," Anna shouted as she grabbed Erika by the shoulders. The female gargoyle had to strain mightily to get them both into the air from a standstill, but she managed it. Obsidian was on the wing next to them. Erika also noticed the Sorceress had taken to the air as well.

Though she wasn't flying away. Instead, she just hovered in the air as she summoned more power.

Erika twisted in Anna's grasp and then reached up and pressed her palms against the female gargoyle's wrists.

"Damn it Erika! I'm trying to save you," Anna shouted.

Erika ignored her and sprinted back toward the Sorceress. Looking up at the female half of the Avatars, she put every bit of will power into making the Sorceress acknowledge her. When the other woman looked down, Erika shouted over the sounds of battle. "What were you saying about there being more to the Divine Ones' plans?"

"It may not matter. We may already be too late. But if you'd have been able to get close to the elemental dragon, I think you would have been able to calm him enough that he'd stay close and allow you to feed on him. If you strip enough of his magic, Gryton may retake command of the body."

"I'll do it."

The Sorceress just shook her head and continued to create the portal spell. "I will not stop you. But I can't guarantee that you'll survive the attempt. He's already so powerful, and you are not yet matured. You may very well die, and I'll still have to send my son to the Spirit Realm. It's not worth your life."

"If I die, I die. According to y'all, it won't be my first time," Erika shouted the words over her shoulder as she began racing toward the three battling titans.

One thing the Sorceress hadn't mentioned was that Erika might die from getting ground into the sand by a certain titan's bigass hooves.

"Watch it!" she shouted up at Lord Draydrak's underbelly as she raced between his legs on her way toward the dragon.

Once she was clear of Draydrak, she sought out the fire elemental.

"Gryton! I'm here. To me!" The soul-link flared once more, and he turned to look at her.

Yes, that's it. Ignore everything and come to me.

The big dragon looked at her but then swung his gaze back to his father.

Behind her, she felt the Sorceress approaching.

"Gregory, let Erika try to help our son. She knows the risks."

A moment later, she felt the weight of the Avatar soul's intense gaze upon her. There was a slight hesitation, then he answered. "Very well. Try to save our son from himself, but don't get killed."

Erika nodded and then glanced over her shoulder and mouthed the words 'thank you' to the Sorceress. Which was probably why she didn't see Gryton bearing down on her position until too late. Within seconds he filled her entire field of vision. The wave of heat hit her before he'd even reached her. Then she was snatched up in one talon tipped hand and the heat intensified tenfold. But by some miracle, that likely had something to do with her powers as a Null, she wasn't burned to a crisp.

Then the dragon surprised her by cradling her protectively against his chest as he turned to face the others on the beach. By his posture, he clearly still considered them threats.

Damn it, he'd never calm with them all standing

around. Then a new idea popped into her head. "Come on. You've got mighty wings. Time to use them."

She wasn't sure if the dragon understood her words or her intent, but suddenly the elemental dragon was spinning on his haunches and then bolting down the beach in a three-legged run. Once he reached the needed speed, he spread his wings wide and then launched himself up into the air. As the beach fell away and the ocean stretched out before them, she was already second-guessing her idea, but there was nothing she could do about that now.

"Let's find some nice island or stretch of the mainland where we can do some hunting. I assume you enjoy hunting, yes? If not, maybe we can sit and talk."

She forced herself to relax with the hope he'd do the same given enough time while she tried not to think about how her plan might be total rubbish. She reassured herself with the knowledge that since the Avatars hadn't followed, it must mean they had faith in her ability to contain Gryton's elemental dragon.

At least, that's what she told herself.

CHAPTER TWO

Lillian

Lillian watched as her son flew swiftly toward the horizon with his Null held protectively in his claws. As if sensing her regard, the dragon dipped closer to the water, making him harder to see. The dragon still raged, and his fire still burned around him, rising up above his scales, but in her heart, she knew the Null would never give up. And neither would her son. They were both survivors.

"He will be fine," her other half acknowledged. "We'll give him and his Null a chance to calm down and then we'll go after them, collect them, and bring them back here to continue with our original purpose for coming."

She smiled up at the other half of her soul. She'd

forgotten how stunning he was when he shed his corporeal form in the Magic Realm. They didn't often have to shed their bodies like he had. But she admitted the wisdom of doing so this time. If Gryton had lost control, her male half could carry their son to the Spirit Realm and then return without harm to himself.

"I should return to my body," he said and then paused before reaching for her. "But first I want to hold my other half for a short time while there is one less bag of flesh between our two halves."

"Bag of flesh. You charmer." But she held her arms out to indicate her willingness. In fact, she was as eager as he was.

One large hand reached down and scooped her up into his palm.

As his magic surrounded her, she could pretend for a time that they were again one being like they were in the Spirit Realm. The only other thing that came close to this sensation of absolute belonging was after a session of powerful lovemaking and her gargoyle mate had still been buried deep within her, their minds and bodies blending together basking in the bliss of shared pleasure.

He chuckled, the sound one of masculine satisfaction. "I hope to experience such a thing again in our future. But for now, I suppose I must return to my flesh and blood body before it dies."

Lillian craned her neck to glare up at him. "Are you telling me you didn't put it in stasis before you started brawling on the beach with our son?"

"There wasn't time. But fear not, I kept enough tethers in place to keep the body alive."

When he lowered her back to the beach, she marched over to his gargoyle body, which was resting in its stone form. She immediately laid her palms against his chest and caressed the stone as she closed her eyes.

With a flick of thought, she weaved a portal spell to the Spirit Realm and redirected the power into her other half, meticulously healing the smallest of damages so he wouldn't feel so much as a twinge of pain at his return.

"You pamper me." He folded his shimmering wings and knelt. Then the other half of her soul began to glimmer more brightly, and his form lost its definition. A moment later, the soul and power of the male half of the Avatars raced into his gargoyle body.

Beneath her hands, his skin warmed and then he was moving, taking her into his arms to give her small delightful gargoyle nips and kisses all along her cheeks and down her neck. When he made to venture lower, following the swell of her breasts, she laughed, smacking him away.

"We have company. Save that thought for later. I'm sure there's something we can do even without our new toys."

Gregory was still laughing in delight as Major Resnick and his team arrived on the back of their gargoyle mounts.

"I saw everything that just happened, and I'm still not sure what I saw," Resnick growled. "And where the fuck did that monster take Private Emerson?"

Lillian turned toward the major and knew she would have to spend some time smoothing ruffled feathers if the alliance had any hope of surviving.

"That was an unfortunate event I wasn't aware was going to happen as neither my Gargoyle Protector nor I have the gift of seeing the future. But one thing I can tell you is that Private Erika Emerson is fine. And my son will be as well once he calms and realizes Erika was never really at risk. Lord Draydrak wasn't planning on harming the Null. He just needed to use her to force out Gryton's dragon. Our son fears that side of himself."

"Wise of him," Sergeant Maracle muttered under his breath. He stood at Resnick's shoulder, his rifle held loose, his body posture surprisingly relaxed as he studied Lord Draydrak. Maracle was one of the most laidback people she'd ever met. Lillian knew an old soul when she saw one. While he wasn't nearly as old as the soul living inside Erika, the sniper of Mohawk heritage was far from young.

Major Resnick cast the man a stern look before returning his full attention back to Lillian. "You're going to start from the beginning and break everything down until I'm satisfied with your answers or this alliance is over."

Lillian bowed to the major. "I shall begin now."

And she did. Even Gregory turned talkative in his effort to help smooth things over. An hour later Major Resnick was still scowling but had calmed.

"Fine. I'll think of something to put in the report that will save the alliance, but we damned well need to get Private Emerson back first."

Lillian nodded and then looked out over the ocean. Distantly she could sense her son. He'd flown very far, very quickly which suggested he was in no mood for company. She looked to Thayn next.

"Old friend, we will need some of your strongest fliers to carry riders that distance."

"Of course."

"Strong, not fast," she added along a private link. *"We need to give Erika time to soothe the dragon."*

He winked at her. *"Only the strongest and the slowest for the Avatars."*

CHAPTER THREE

Erika

The elemental dragon had flown swiftly away from Lord Death's kingdom, wings beating tirelessly. After the first half-hour, Erika had noticed the dragon's body had cooled significantly. She hoped that meant he was regaining control of his elemental fire.

"Gryton, can you hear me?" She attempted the words verbally first since she wasn't sure what would happen if she tried to use the soul link to touch his thoughts. If the dragon was still all instincts and rages, he might think it another type of attack.

But just then the big dragon flexed his neck and focused one giant eyeball upon her.

"Hey, you did hear me." She patted one of his claws. "That's good. We're making progress."

Or at least she thought they were until he looked ahead again.

"Or not." She scowled at him, and then tried to wiggle enough that she could see more of their surroundings through a crack between two of his fingers. All she saw was the sky. With a huff, she sat back down.

"Oh, come on. I know you might not be able to talk in this form, but you've spoken in my mind in the past. "Say something. Anything?"

He continued his flight. Sighing, Erika settled back down to wait and decided the silver lining in all this was that she didn't have to pee. He flew for another hour, and eventually, she relaxed against the warm scales of his chest.

"I'm trusting you here," she told him.

And it was a moment of trust because if he shifted his foreclaw away from his chest, she'd fall to her death. Or if they weren't high enough that the fall would kill her, she'd have drowning to look forward to. But he didn't drop her, and eventually, she dozed.

Sometime later, she jerked awake to find him banking in the air.

Shouting, she scrambled at his fingers, hoping to secure herself in some way as her body tipped forward. He slowed even more and then reared until he was almost vertical.

"Whoa! Easy!" But then there was only a slight jolt as he came in for a landing.

Heart pounding, she dragged in calming breaths and decided it was good to be on solid ground even if she couldn't see it. Soon she wondered where they were and what she was supposed to do now. The dragon seemed calmer, his power levels mellower, but it was hard to gauge if he'd sustained physical damage in the fight, which might explain the diminished amount of magic he was giving off. But he *had* been able to fly this far, so he probably wasn't too damaged—physically.

Magically and mentally? That was to be determined.

The narrow strips of light between his fingers grew in size, and then he was lifting her away from his chest and placing her on the ground.

She glanced around. They were on a large island, or perhaps this was still the mainland, just far from where the forward operating base was being set up.

A rocky beach led up to steep cliffs. She craned her neck.

"Oh, look. More forest." There didn't seem to be a speck of civilization for miles. Though that might be a good thing if the dragon was still twitchy. The last thing he needed was another fight.

She turned back to the dragon. He was just as big as she remembered, but now his scales were more of a shimmering bronze with a hint of flame-red color at the edges. As far as she could see, there were no open wounds or fire anywhere. And no flames dripping out his mouth had to be a good sign.

She leaned back to meet his eyes. "Howdy."

The dragon huffed and lowered his long, narrow head toward her.

"Please don't be about to eat me. Not one of the ways I want to go out."

But he didn't. Instead, he sniffed at her, nuzzling her gently. He had two long whiskery tendrils growing from the ridges above both nostrils and several shorter ones lining the underside of his jaw. They wiggled rather like a cat's whiskers as he sniffed her. It wasn't until a bright red forked tongue flicked out that she realized he was tasting the magic she was radiating.

"The magic isn't a weapon, I promise."

The dragon snorted out what might have been a humorous 'I know that' before he continued to nuzzle and inhale her scent.

"You're drinking the magic I'm giving off, aren't you?" She was pretty sure he was. "You sure that's a good idea? Just a little while ago, you were dangerously close to losing control of all that fire magic."

He huffed at her again, and this time he actually rolled an eye at her.

"Well, I'm glad one of us knows what we're doing." Her words seemed to please the beast even more, and he puffed up his chest and arched his neck as the rest of his body coiled around her.

It was the first time she realized how long and sleekly built he was. Other than his powerful chest, which was likely developed to that extent to power flight, he was long, slim, and trim. He was positively elegant for such a large creature. His long, snake-like tail coiled around his body and then the tip wrapped around her.

"Ease up there, big fella. I'm not going anywhere, and I really don't need you squeezing hard enough to pop my eyeballs right out of my head."

He loosened his tail enough that she could draw in a deep breath without cracking a rib.

"Hah. You really can understand me." She tilted her head inquiringly. "Now what?"

He lowered his head until it rested on the ground. Then he just studied her. After another fifteen minutes of staring, his eyes slowly drifted close.

"Uh-oh. Wait one minute. If it's nap time, I want a safer place to nap. I don't want to die by you rolling on me in your sleep."

His eye blinked open and he snorted in what she was coming to understand was humor. The dark eye with a vertical pupil peered at her for a moment, and then the lids drifted closed again.

Erika patted the topmost coil of his tail with a bit more force than might have been wise, but she wanted him to know of her dissatisfaction. When he blinked his eye back open, she gentled her patting.

"If it's nap time, is there any chance I can stretch out on the ground. Humans don't sleep standing up, you know?"

He regarded her for a moment as if she was asking a lot of him, but slowly his coils shifted, opening up a space large enough she could recline. After a brief pause, she did just that. No point annoying the dragon, or he might take away the extra space.

She wouldn't sleep, but she'd indulge the dragon and see if he'd fall asleep and then once he was out, she'd try climbing over his coils to have a look around. But as she lay there looking up at the darkening sky, she realized she was tired. It had been a long day by any standard.

When the dragon shifted, she jerked back to full wakefulness, fearing he was already asleep and about to crush her, but the eye facing her was open once more. Suddenly the tip of his long tail gently inserted itself between her head and the hard ground.

Oh...was he really making a pillow out of his tail for her? That was sweet and totally not something Gryton would worry about.

"Thanks, Big Guy," she said because her grandad always said you should appreciate hospitality when it was offered.

After another yawn, she relaxed as much as she was able on the hard ground and soon her own eyes were drifting closed.

CHAPTER FOUR

Erika

Thirst was the first thing to register on her consciousness. It might even have been thirst that woke her from sleep. She rolled over and looked around. Above her, the sky was already brightening with dawn. Her slight movement must have woken the dragon too, for his nearest eye was open and watching her.

Standing slowly, she studied him for a response. When she didn't get one, she walked closer to his head. As she approached, she even dared to run her fingers along the scales of his neck. He didn't react to that touch, so she determined he was in a pretty mellow mood.

"Morning. Any chance you'll let me go find some potable water and maybe a place to pee in privacy?"

He huffed again. This was softer than his humor one, so

she thought it might be a 'yes' to her question. A moment later, the dragon uncoiled from around her. She immediately noticed what was missing.

"Where the hell did your wings go?" She stood on her toes, trying to get a better look. "We're going to be needing them to get back home."

He arched his neck and glanced over his shoulder at his bare back as if he found her question perplexing. But he made no attempt to answer her question. Instead he rose and shook himself, dislodging pebbles and sand from his bronze hide.

Actually, now under the morning light, he looked a different color again, more like a fire's embers, dark at the base of each scale lightening as the scale proceeded to the tip. As he moved, the scales seemed to pulse with a soft glow in time to his breathing. It reminded her of the tattoo Gryton had had on his chest.

"The tattoo you had when you looked human," she gestured at her own chest. "Gryton said it was a representation of his true name. But what he really meant was that it was your name. It's a visual representation of you, like your coloration or the color and type of magic you command or something along those lines, isn't it?"

Once again, the dragon didn't answer her. Instead he merely started off down the rocky beach. When she didn't immediately follow, he turned and looked back.

"Oh, you want me to follow. Why didn't you say so?" She rolled her eyes and started after him.

It wasn't long before she heard falling water. "Oh, God in Heaven, that has to be fresh water if there's a waterfall."

She hurried her steps, running to catch up with the

dragon. And sure enough, it was a small waterfall rushing over the side of the cliff high above her head. She approached closer, not caring that she was getting sprayed.

Bending, she dipped her hands in the fresh water. She was so thirsty; she was tempted to just gulp it down but paused to grab the purification tabs from their pocket. Of course she didn't have a container. She glanced up at the dragon, but it wasn't like he'd have anything hidden behind his scales that would be useful for her, so she ripped open the package. She held the tab between her teeth while she scooped up a large handful of water and then awkwardly dropped the tab into her waiting hands.

The most difficult task of her life may have been keeping the water from leaking out between her fingers for the required time. After fifteen minutes, she lost patience and lowered her head and drank. All the while she felt the dragon watching her. The water was probably safe, and he likely thought her an idiot for not trusting him, but she wasn't going to risk picking up some nasty alien bacteria from the water. There would be no horror movie alien busting out of any part of Private Emerson, thank you very much.

After she'd drained the water from her hands, she looked up at the dragon.

"Thanks for leading me here, but now I need to pee, so be a nice, polite dragon and stay here while I move a little way down the beach to that nice pile of rocks over there." She waved her hand in the direction.

When he didn't do anything, she took that as permission and made her way over to the rocks and attended to nature. Once she was finished, she returned to the dragon to find him bathing—or maybe that was playing—under the waterfall. Erika watched him as she knelt down and washed her hands in the stream flowing into the ocean.

"You being a fire elemental and all, it never occurred to me you would like water. Gryton didn't even have to bathe. He didn't stink, and I'm pretty sure he just used his elemental fire to purify his body."

The dragon paused in his play and then his tail whipped out of the water, sending a wave of it in Erika's direction. She shrieked in surprise and attempted to duck, which did absolutely nothing to protect her from the onslaught of water that hit her.

"Thanks a lot!" She growled at him and then scowled for good measure.

The dragon flicked more water at her and then pointed his muzzle at the small pool. His two longest whiskers trailed in the water as if trying to communicate something to her.

She glanced down at herself and then over at the dragon in the pool. Raising one arm, she gave herself a sniff. Ugh. Yep, not so fresh. "Ah hell, you're trying to tell me I stink."

She approached the pool and then looked up at the dragon with narrowed eyes.

"You better not be doing this just to get me naked," she said in jest as she started shedding her gear.

Casting a subtle glance toward his underbelly, she studied the region but didn't see any equipment or telltale bulges there, then remembered what he'd said about being neither male nor female when he'd first been born. Perhaps the dragon was genderless still.

She shrugged, stripped out of her clothing, and stepped into the pool. The water was cool but not cold. There was no danger of hypothermia and the day felt like a summer morning though she couldn't guess what season it was here on this alien world. Maybe it was always like summer here, or they were in a tropical location. The trees looked like a strange mix of conifers and deciduous. Though the plentiful numbers of thick, fleshy vines suggested tropical vegetation.

With another shrug, she put it out of her mind and grabbed handfuls of sand to scrub herself with. Some soap or any kind of supplies would have been nice, but sometime between the time Lord Draydrak had caught her and when the dragon had snatched her up, her pack had been ripped away, the straps shredded by someone's claws.

Once she was finished, she glanced up at the dragon to find him watching her.

"You been watching me the entire time?" *Why you great perverted beast.*

The dragon smirked, and she suddenly wondered if he'd been in her head this entire time and she just couldn't detect him. If so, it stood to reason that he was even more powerful than Gryton. Not the most comforting thought.

"Fine. Enjoy my lily-white ass. She turned and grabbed her clothing and pulled on the sports bra and pants before kneeling at the edge of the pool to scrub her shirt. Her attire was a little rough from getting manhandled by demigods, but it was still serviceable with a little more cleaning.

She eyed the dragon, hoping after a day in the wilds he would calm enough to relinquish his hold and allow Gryton to return. Not for the first time she wished she had her radio, but that had been lost at some point as well.

She dragged on the rest of her still wet clothing. It was warm enough they should dry unless she got the complementary dragon rinse cycle again. Glancing back at the dragon where he was coiling himself on a large rock to sunbathe, she snorted.

"Oh no, you don't. I'm hungry. Food first and then you can sunbathe to your heart's content."

Looking unimpressed at her words, the dragon grunted and hoisted himself back to his feet and started off down the beach. He paused and looked over his shoulder, repeating what he'd done earlier.

"I'm coming. Don't get your knickers in a knot. My legs are way shorter than yours." All the same, she hurried to catch up. The faster she moved, the sooner she'd eat.

It wasn't until they reached a section where the beach vanished and the cliff wall met the ocean, that Erika slowed. But the dragon didn't. He started up the side of the cliff wall like he was walking on flat ground.

"There's no way I can do that." If she had ropes for climbing, she could do the ascent in an hour or so. Depending. But she wasn't about to do it without a line.

The dragon was twenty feet up when the end of his tail slid past her. Then in the next moment, she was being wrapped by the vice-like appendage and being hoisted up the side of the cliff.

Screaming and wailing like some chickenshit on a rollercoaster, it certainly wasn't one of her finer moments, but she and the dragon made it to the top of the cliff, and soon she was in the forest.

"Hey. You can put me down now. I can walk."

He partly did as she asked as his tail deposited her just behind his head. She found herself straddling his neck. Reaching forward, she grabbed fistfuls of his spiky mane. She would have grabbed one of his horns for a more secure grip, but they were too far above her head. Besides, they moved every time his head did.

Slowly she grew used to his gait. While riding dragon back was vastly different than horseback, the concept of moving with the body between her legs was the same. He continued his swift mode of travel until he came to a break in the trees. It wasn't a large clearing, but there was enough space for her to build a fire in the center and the dragon still to have room to recline along the edge next to the fallen tree.

With a bit of disappointment, she realized this was the end of their journey, and she'd been enjoying the ride.

Oh well. She was hungry.

He lowered his head until it was only about three feet off the ground. She kicked her one leg over his neck and slid down. Dragon dismount completed in a somewhat elegant fashion, she walked the area and picked out a patch of rocky ground where she could build a cooking fire with a little effort.

The dragon paused to watch her for a moment.

"Don't worry. I'll stay here until you return. You have my word, Lord Dragon." She gave the dragon a courtly little bow.

The dragon chuckled, steam rolling out of his mouth as he laughed. He was still chuckling as he vanished between the trees. She watched the spot where he'd been for a few minutes and then turned to prepare her cooking fire.

He'd be back. She was sure of it.

CHAPTER FIVE

Erika

Her trust in the dragon wasn't misplaced. Less than a half-hour later, he returned with an alien buck in his jaws. Well, it looked like a deer, and it was male, so buck it was. If she wasn't misreading the dragon, he was acting more than a little proud when he presented her with the deer.

"Nice job." It was only natural to reach out and rub him in reward as if he was a loyal hunting hound.

The dragon didn't take exception. In fact, he seemed to like the attention, leaning in for more of a scratch. She put her weight behind it and gave him a good rubbing. It was only then that she noticed something odd.

"I'm not feeding or radiating power. That's a first." She eyed the dragon. "You got something to do with that?"

The dragon didn't answer, instead nudging the carcass of the deer.

"All right. You're hungry too. Let me just cut myself a portion, and the rest of it is all yours."

After she'd butchered the deer and taken the choicest cut—because really, she was certain he was just going to gulp the whole thing down—she brought her meat over to the cooking fire. The wood had burned down to beautiful coals, and she suspended the meat on twigs she'd already stripped of bark for the task.

By the time she turned back to the dragon, the buck was gone. Not a speck of it remained.

"Wow. Dragons aren't picky eaters, are you?" Then she realized he was a fire elemental, so maybe everything was just fuel for him. "Could eating tree branches keep you alive, I wonder?"

The dragon looked at her and then the nearest tree. His serpentine head snaked out and powerful jaws snapped closed on a branch, severing it from the trunk. Three bites later, the branch was gone.

"Wow. Seriously, no need to eat wood if you have other preferences. I was just curious."

She continued to talk to the dragon but fell silent after a while, tired of keeping up the one-sided conversation. The dragon seemed comfortable with the silence, and so too was she. As surreal as camping with a dragon should seem, it felt kind of natural. It was certainly much more relaxing than it would have been to sit across a fire from Gryton.

She stretched and wished she had a camp chair or something to lean against. Sitting cross-legged was never her favorite position, but it wasn't like the dragon could magic up a chair, and she didn't plan to rough it in the forest long enough to make one.

Eyeing the dragon, she smirked as an idea formed. While he might not be able to magic-up a chair, he might fill the same function. She adjusted the meat over the fire and then stood and stretched again.

Approaching the dragon in a leisurely fashion, she gave him a friendly smile. "Mind if I join you on this side of the fire?"

When he didn't do anything more than tilt his head in her direction, she settled down next to his scale-covered belly and then scooted closer to use him as a backrest. She had a moment of doubt at the wisdom of her decision when he shifted, but he only curled the tip of his tail over her lap, rather like a warm, fleshy seatbelt.

She traced the pattern of fine scales under her fingers. Her hunch proved correct. He was a tactile creature and started to rumble in what she was pretty sure was happiness.

"You're really rather sweet. Just between you and me, I have to admit to liking you more than Gryton."

A deep rumbling emerged from his chest at her words. She looked away from the tail she was rubbing and turned her head to face his. His eyes were open, and his lips curled slightly at the corners. Was he smiling?

Yes, she was pretty sure that was a dragon smile. Wisps of steam escaped between his teeth, and she was reminded that he was also dangerous. But then so was Gryton. She hadn't feared him, and she didn't fear the dragon either.

Though she would like it if he would communicate with

her in some way because they did need to have a conversation about their futures. She sensed the dragon could likely be more volatile than Gryton. Actually, the dragon's earlier actions proved as much. Perhaps she could somehow convince both personalities to share time in control of the body. That would be the best of both worlds.

Gryton when they need strategy and cunning; the dragon when they needed to fight.

The dragon's muzzle moved closer and brushed her in what was clearly a nuzzle of affection. She laughed. She couldn't help herself. Attempting to fend him off, she braced her hands against his muzzle and pushed for all she was worth, but it was like trying to move a concrete wall.

"Okay. You win." She allowed the dragon to have his way. It wasn't until a mellow warmth began to rise from her skin that she realized he was somehow stimulating her gift into releasing some stored-up magic.

That was new. She wasn't aware she could just store it like a battery. Or that he, or perhaps others, could trigger her into releasing that stored up power. That could come in handy if some of the magic wielders needed to do a big fancy spell back on Earth.

The dragon's two longest feelers brushed against her shoulders and up into her hair for a moment before brushing back down over her chest.

"You better not be getting fresh with me," she said in jest, knowing he wasn't. While she couldn't read his thoughts like she could Gryton's, she was beginning to pick up little bits of emotion that bled off the dragon.

He was familiarizing himself with her scent. Though she sensed there was more to it. They shared a soul link.

Then something else occurred to her. What if he wanted the piece of his soul back?

That was a scary thought, but she calmed herself a moment later. If the dragon wanted the soul shard back, he'd had ample time to tear it out of her chest with those big claws of his.

No, this was something else. He wanted something else.

"You're lonely, aren't you? Gryton was too, though he'd die before admitting as much." She reached up and stroked her fingers down the dragon's muzzle. "You are unique in the universe. It's only natural that you'd be lonely. I might not be anything as grand as you, but I'll offer you the same deal I was going to offer Gryton if he was less of a prickly asshole. I'll be your friend if you want."

Her words seemed to please the dragon for he rumbled in that happy way and affectionately rubbed his nose against her chest.

"Easy! You're going to break ribs." The dragon understood and eased up. After a time, he pulled back and then just sat and watched the tiny flames that occasionally burst to life from the edges of the glowing coals.

That reminded Erika to attend to her meal. Now that the dragon wasn't taking up all her senses, she took note of the divine smell of the juices cooking out of the meat and hitting the coals. She loved the smell of food cooking over open flames. Heck, she just loved the smell of a campfire, the sight and sound of the flames.

She gently pushed the dragons tail aside and got up to turn the meat. She'd rescued it just in time. Before long, it was finished, and she was blowing on it to cool. After she ate her fill, the dragon led her to a stream to quench her thirst before they returned to the fire.

"So," she asked him in a companionable tone, "how long do you plan to stay here? As much as I love camping, we have duties to perform. Besides, you can't stay in dragon form forever. Eventually, you'll have to allow Gryton to have his body back."

The dragon jerked upright from where he'd been lazing next to the fire.

Shit. She'd hit a nerve with that last comment.

Turning his back to her, he flopped his butt back down on the ground and looked out into the forest, away from her. His tail was coiled, the tip shaking in warning like a rattlesnake about to strike.

Mentally questioning what she was about to do, she stood up and brushed the leaf litter off herself and then started toward the dragon. When she approached him from the side and caught the attention of the nearest eye, he suddenly shifted his butt, so he was fully facing away from her again.

She fought back a smirk, knowing she shouldn't be laughing, but it was still hilarious. He was just so big and aloof looking, he reminded her of an angry cat butt-hurt over some insult.

"Hey, I'm sorry. It's nothing about you lacking anything. I think you're just about the most awesome thing I've ever laid eyes on." To her surprise, she found the words were entirely true. "And if we didn't have pressing matters that needed our attention, I would be more than happy for you to remain as you are and camp with you for the next month, but fate waits for no one."

She placed a hand on the dragon's side. He shifted again, turning away once more.

"Oh, alright. Let's not ruin our new friendship over this. If you don't want to return to the form you wore as Gryton, I understand. This is your true form, after all. I'll never make you change what you are. Forgive me?"

The dragon stood ramrod straight for another ten seconds, then he relaxed his posture and curled his tail around her waist. With a little urging, she got him to sit next to the fire with her.

She patted his tail. "There, see? Forgiveness is easy, isn't it?"

The dragon rumbled, though she didn't know if it was agreement or disagreement.

Moved by some urge she didn't truly understand, she leaned forward and pressed a kiss to the dragon's cheek. The warmth and peace that flowed through her soul reminded her of what it had been like to hug her dog. She'd had to leave Baxter with her granddad when she'd joined up, and that had been one of the hardest things she'd ever done.

Sitting here with the dragon was a little like sitting next to a campfire back home, with her dog's head in her lap and her horse grazing in a corral as her grandad sat across the fire and told stories of his youthful escapades.

"God, I miss them sometimes."

The dragon lowered his muzzle, his tongue flicking out and tasting the single tear that rolled down her cheek.

At the touch, their soul-link flared full and a mellow warmth washed over her, and she felt loved. She didn't know what the dragon thought at this moment, but she was pretty confident he was trying to tell her that she wasn't alone.

She closed her eyes, her lids suddenly too heavy to keep open. Sleep was just rising up to snatch her when a voice rumbled in her mind. *"You are mine and will never know loneliness again after we become one."*

She frowned in her sleep. The dragon meant the words to be comforting, but something in the tone sent a shiver down her spine and nightmares chased her in her dreams afterward.

CHAPTER SIX

Vaspara

Only the harpy's strong arm around her waist kept Vaspara on her feet. And even then, she stumbled more often than she walked under her own power. She hurt so much all she wanted was to crumple to the ground, but her will to live, to see Sorac and the draklings again—and Bervicta's stubborn refusal to release her—were all too strong to willingly give in to death.

But a body, even a half-demon body, could only be pushed so far.

"I need to rest."

"No. You rest, you die. If we don't get you to Sorac before the sun sets, you probably won't live to see another one."

"I've had worse."

"Maybe. But those times Sorac was there to make sure you fed and grew strong once more." The harpy chuckled, managing to find humor even in this. "Sorac was a good nursemaid. Did you ever notice how swiftly handsome males presented themselves outside the healer's quarters anytime you were hurt?"

Vaspara tried to focus on her friend's words. "I was their captain. I treated them well. They were loyal."

"Yes. And did you know they'd fight for the privilege of having you feed on them? The biggest, most muscle-bound troll would have won if Sorac hadn't stepped in and selected your feeding partners the times you were too delirious with pain and hunger to be able to choose your own male."

"I didn't know that."

"He always selected the prettiest, the most intelligent, and the most skilled of lovers. Heck if I know how he picked the best ones."

"And how would you know they were the best lovers?" Vaspara managed to give Bervicta a broken half-grin. The other half of her mouth was twisted, puffy, and refused to move.

The harpy cleared her throat. "I may have sampled a few of them at a later date to see the reason Sorac had picked them for you. I never knew why he'd didn't choose the worst lovers to increase the likelihood you'd pick him instead, but he never did."

"Sorac is too honorable to act in a deceitful way."

"Yes. But still. Picking out superb lovers for the woman

he loved—that's love in its most devoted form. Can you imagine doing the same—picking females to sleep in your beloved's bed?"

"I would have done the same for him no matter how much it hurt."

"See. My point. True love. You both caught the disease."

Vaspara didn't deny her friend's words. She just hoped she lived long enough to see Sorac again so she could tell him she loved him one last time. Because even if she saw Sorac again, the Battle Goddess would never allow them to come together as lovers. And Vaspara doubted if the demigoddess would allow the djinn to share power with her.

Vaspara had outlived her usefulness, and while she carried news of a Null with her, she doubted if even that would be enough to sway the Battle Goddess into allowing her to live.

She was jolted out of her thoughts by an ear throbbing roar. It came a second time before the first was finished echoing through the mountain valley they were traversing. Vaspara looked up, but her vision swam and black crept in from the edges. She couldn't see anything, but she knew that roar. She'd heard it on the battlefield enough times.

"Sorac!" But it couldn't be. They weren't close enough to the fortress to hear him.

She breathed through her mouth, deep calming breaths, and slowly her vision cleared somewhat. It was still blurry, but she could make out shapes. And a sizeable dark form was racing through the sky toward her location. "That's not possible."

The harpy gave Vaspara a squeeze. "I called to Sorac along a private link as soon as we crossed the portal from the Mortal Realm. All the captains have the power to command him, but I also shouted at the others to allow him to come to us, that we carried valuable information about a newly discovered Null."

"The Battle Goddess will be enraged that you called Sorac to aid me."

"I didn't call him to aid you. I called him to aid me getting valuable information to the Battle Goddess before you die. If you die, your memories die with you, and our goddess will not know how powerful this Null is or even have a description of her. So, you see? Calling Sorac is entirely to make me look better in our demigoddess's eyes."

"You're a terrible liar." Vaspara started to laugh and then gasped in pain. "Goddess, don't make me laugh."

But then there was no more time for banter. Sorac was there, spreading his mighty wings wide to slow himself enough that he could scoop them up in his claws. Vaspara screamed at the slight impact, and her beloved firedrake echoed her pain with anguish of his own.

"I'm so sorry, my beloved," he said, worry for her making his voice shake and slur some of the words.

"It's all right. You're here." *I can die now if the Divine Ones have decided my time is over.*

"Don't you dare!" Sorac roared as he beat his wings, rising into the sky faster than she'd ever seen him climb. He arrowed straight up for thirty powerful sweeps of his mighty wings, then he leveled out and raced toward the fortress city.

Cradled in his clawed hands, she felt safe and loved. She

drifted away then only to be drawn back by the firedrake's anguished cries and Bervicta's shouted words telling her that if she died, the harpy would curse her. Underlaying the harsh words was a plea to live for her close friend.

She continued to drift, her senses dulling further until only her hearing remained.

"She's a mess," the Battle Goddess commented. "You say Gryton and a Null did this?"

"Yes." Bervicta's one-word answer was clipped.

"The mission wasn't a complete failure then. If you and she hadn't made it back, we never would have known about this new dangerous complication." The Battle Goddess paused. "Did she happen to mention anything about the Null? Strength? Species? Even gender?"

"Nothing beyond mentioning the Null was female, my Goddess. There wasn't time, and then by the time Sorac reached us, it was too late. She'd lost consciousness. If she dies, we'll never learn the identity of this new threat. The Null could be any female member of the Light's army, and we'd never know until too late."

"Harpy, you don't have to convince me to save your friend's life. I'm aware of how valuable the news Vaspara carries is. Bring her a male so she may feed."

Vaspara kept her eyes closed. Actually, she wasn't sure if she could even open them. Not that it mattered. The others continued to talk about her like she wasn't there.

"My Goddess," the harpy began, sounding as polite as Vaspara had ever heard her. "I'm not sure if she can even rally herself to feed on a normal male, but Sorac is the son of a fertility deity. Perhaps he can do something to begin her healing."

"The firedrake and the succubus are never to see each other again." The accompanying rattle of chains suggested the Battle Goddess was moving away.

"Sorac is raging. Taryin is already looking strained. If Sorac puts up enough fight—and he won't stop until he is dead—the djinn will use this distraction to slip the blood witch's control. Though I suppose you could always order the djinn to kill Sorac and risk a civil war."

Chains rattled louder and then there was the sound of flesh hitting flesh, followed by a moment of silence which in turn was terminated by the sound of a body—Bervicta's —hitting the wall on the other side of the great hall.

A groan and a curse were followed by the scent of blood. A moment later, she heard Bervicta spit on the floor.

"Taryin, release Sorac before you get us all killed." The Battle Goddess's words were hard and cold and utterly surprising. And they only turned more deadly by the word. "Harpy. This is your last warning. Learn your place, or I'll let the witch have you."

"I serve at the pleasure of my Goddess," Bervicta said, the last word ending on a wheeze. She'd likely broken ribs on impact, and at least one had pierced a lung to go by the wet sound of her breaths.

Still unable to use most of her senses, Vaspara couldn't determine what other injuries the harpy had sustained. She knew her friend was tough and would quickly recover from the damage. But if Bervicta kept defending her and Sorac, the harpy's luck would run out.

She also knew how stubborn the harpy was. Telling her to stop would do no good.

"And Bervicta," menace echoed through the vast chamber as the Battle Goddess bit out the words, "if Sorac manages to escape with Vaspara, I will kill you slowly."

"I would expect nothing less."

"Get out of my sight." There was another long pause as Vaspara felt the Battle Goddess's gaze upon her. "And take that burnt piece of meat with you. Return her only after she's fully healed and able to stand up to some questioning."

"At once, my Goddess!" The sound of boots announced Bervicta's approach. Then two hands closed over Vaspara's wrists, and she was unceremoniously dragged from the chamber. It wasn't until they turned down two lengths of corridors that Bervicta stopped and lifted her up in her arms.

"I'm sorry for the rough handling, but it seems I've tested the Battle Goddess as much as I dare. I'll take you to Sorac's old rooms. I've already ordered soldiers from my battalion to escort Sorac to you as quickly as possible. He'll be here soon."

"Thank you." She had trouble getting the second word out, her mouth was so dry.

"Save your thanks until after the Battle Goddess has finished her questioning. You may want to punch me more than thank me."

Vaspara would have laughed, but she didn't think she had enough breath left in her lungs for that.

They'd almost reached Sorac's chambers when they heard pounding footsteps running up behind them. Bervicta twisted to face the newcomers, and suddenly

Vaspara was being lifted from one set of arms to a larger more powerful set.

"Oh, my beloved. I'm so sorry. I fought and tried to come to you but couldn't break free."

"She knows. And she also knows you love her, and she loves you. And back and forth and forth and back. Now get to the kissing and fucking part before we lose her."

"Set your soldiers to guard the hallway and chambers," Sorac ordered as he started forward. "You come with us. If you're in close enough proximity to me when I heal Vaspara, you'll be healed as well."

"Don't waste your energy on me."

"Vaspara is weak. And this will have to be a long, slow healing. There will be a lot of magic cast off that she won't be able to absorb, but you might as well put it to good use."

"Fine. As long as you aren't trying to form a harem."

Sorac snorted. "Vaspara is enough for any man."

"Good. Because while your draklings are cute, I certainly wouldn't want to have to pop out one of the bleeding eggs first."

Even just being held in Sorac's arms helped. Vaspara was nowhere near recovered, but she was able to force her eyelids open. Though only a few blurry shapes took form.

Soft lips brushed the skin above her left eye. It was a relatively undamaged bit of skin. Sorac continued along her brow to her temple and then along her hairline to her ear. His nipping little kisses moved to the column of her neck and everywhere his lips brushed, power washed across her.

But it wasn't enough. She was desperate for more.

"Soon," he promised. "Just as soon as I get this armor off you."

He was even more gentle than his words had implied as he freed her of her armor. And his lovemaking was equally as gentle. By the end of the first round that had her chanting his name as she clung to him, she was already beginning to recover, but Sorac had no plans to stop until he'd healed every scratch.

CHAPTER SEVEN

Gryton

His senses were already awake and sending him information before his conscious mind had thoroughly roused. Gryton drew in a deep breath, and the scent of a human tickled his nose. It wasn't unpleasant. The human servants in the Battle Goddess's kingdom were required to practice proper hygiene along with the rest of her army.

She prided herself on being civilized and delivering all the benefits of the empire to the newly conquered kingdoms.

However, whether a human servant bathed had no bearing on his present situation, because there were precisely zero reasons why he should be waking up next to a human. Come to think of it, he couldn't remember the last time he'd surrendered his consciousness to sleep like many mortals or immortals were required to do by their inferior physiology. It usually only happened after he'd been wounded in a battle and he needed to go into a deep meditative state to regain control over his raging fire magic.

But even that wasn't like actual sleep.

And this most certainly felt like what he'd seen in the minds of others as they woke.

He wondered which of his rivals—it had to be one of the captains playing a jest on him—had gotten the upper hand and somehow bewitched him into mating with a human female. The female was lucky not to get burned to a crisp. If he were to guess, this was some prank of Sorac's making.

Once he got his hands on the firedrake—

"Hey, you shifted back," said a husky and strangely familiar voice, though he couldn't connect a face to it.

He snapped his eyes open and found himself looking into his bedpartner's gaze. Her eyes were familiar, and so was the sucking sensation drawing his magic away. And that was sufficient to finally trigger his reluctant memory.

The Null.

Why was he sleeping with Erika? What was going on?

There was a suspicious draft along his back from neck to ankles. He was most certainly naked. What had possessed him? He couldn't remember anything, and now he was looking into the Null's eyes.

Had they really had sex, and she'd sucked him dry? He remembered the time she'd joked about it. But now it wasn't humorous. She'd somehow taken his memories along with his magic.

"You don't remember anything, do you?" She leaned back and looked down at him. "Oh, my God! You're naked."

She rolled away from him, and they both leaped to their feet at the same time. Erika stood with one hand over her eyes and the other trying to block out her non-existent view of his nether regions.

Her reaction would have been comical if he hadn't had his memory stolen from him.

"Mortal, explain what has happened." He laced his voice with threat.

She peered between her fingers and then made a pained sound.

"Cover that up." She waved her hand in the general direction of his waist.

He noticed she was fully clothed. "We didn't mate?"

"What? Heck no! Why would you think that?"

He gestured at himself to indicate his present state of undress and then added, "I don't remember anything after Lord Draydrak snatched you up."

"And you just leaped to the conclusion we had sex and it was so terrible you blocked it like a traumatic event?"

He grimaced. "I thought your powers as a Null may have stolen more than my magic and taken my memories."

"Well, that wasn't what happened." She paused and then glanced in his direction, keeping her gaze on his face.

With a grunt, he called back his protective armor. As it flowed across his body, he turned his attention back to the Null. "Well, what happened then?"

"You turned into a dragon."

"What!"

"You really don't remember that?"

"I—" He paused and scoured his mind. He detected no lie in the Null's thoughts. Now that he knew what he needed to look for, he swiftly found a knot of memories cordoned off from the rest of his mind. It only took a little prod, and then they were merging with the rest of his memories.

He braced himself as they rushed over him, events unfolding at many times the normal pace until he'd experienced everything. After it was over, he released a shaky breath.

"You okay?" Erika asked him.

"No."

When Lord Draydrak had snatched up Erika and said he was going to kill her, Gryton's fear and rage had merged into a cold kind of power that burned with purpose. Within heartbeats, the dragon had risen within him and ripped its way through every safeguard and layer of protection he put in place to keep it caged.

The dragon had broken free all because it feared for the Null's life. But it wasn't the only one panicked at the thought of Erika's death. The thought of the Null no longer beside him, nattering in his ear about some nonsense or other, left him feeling empty and aching and horrified. That disturbed him almost as much as the ease with which the dragon was able to circumvent all Gryton's protections in his moment of weakness.

He closed his eyes as he processed all that had happened in a little over a day.

But he had the dragon's memories and the emotions it had felt as each event had unfolded.

The memories also clearly showed that Erika liked the dragon. She was more at ease with the beast than with him. But she had no clue of the creature's mind, the depth of its possessive nature. Or how powerful it truly was. Gryton discovered a new power he possessed, or perhaps it was only an ability the dragon's ruthlessness could channel. But it could kill with a mere thought, burning away a weaker adversary's mind from within.

That's why it hadn't touched the Null's thoughts using their soul-link. The beast didn't want to damage his prized one. That was how the dragon thought of her—his precious one, his dear one, his beautiful weapon.

But the dragon revealed none of these things to the Null. It was waiting for her to finish maturing. But when she did, the dragon had plans. Plans Gryton couldn't allow it to achieve.

It wished to merge consciousnesses with the Null, to combine their very souls together into one being. Like the Avatars, or like what Anna and Obsidian might grow into given time.

Terror—a sensation he'd never felt until Lord Draydrak snatched up the Null—stirred in his heart and mind again. This time it was at the thought of what would become of Erika's soul when his dragon managed to seduce her and devoured her soul and merged it with its own.

Gryton told himself it wasn't because he cared for Erika that he wished to protect her from the dragon. He would do the same for any Null in order to prevent the dragon from combining two of the greatest powers in the universe into one deadly, near undefeatable force.

A Null was immune to magical attack, but that wasn't the weapon the dragon was bringing to bear against Erika. It was being charming. And, strangely, Gryton detected no falsehoods in the dragon's memories. It really did like her in an honest, uncomplicated way. But Gryton knew it wouldn't stop there.

The dragon's every thought was tinted with possessiveness.

It thought of Erika as 'mine' as clearly as if the dragon had scent marked her for all to smell.

"Hey, Hot Stuff. Are you okay?"

He opened his eyes and glowered at her. "I'll be fine as soon as you stop feeding on me."

Her eyes widened and then narrowed again. "If I was feeding, it was because you were feeling antsy about something. I assume it's the whole 'shifting into dragon form' that's got you all riled up."

She didn't know how close she'd come to hitting upon the truth.

"We'll talk more about this later. We're about to get company." Though in truth, Gryton had no plans to share any of his fears with her. He'd battle the dragon alone as he always had. Eventually, he'd win. Or die trying.

CHAPTER EIGHT

Erika

The Avatars in the company of Major Resnick and the rest of the team arrived before Erika could get to the meat of the matter with Gryton. But she'd soon shoved her questions about the dragon aside for later and had begun doing what she could to smooth things over before the dragon decided he needed to put in another appearance.

As much as she liked the dragon, she'd gotten the impression from Gryton that the dragon wouldn't be as cute and cozy with others as it had been with her. But luckily, things went relatively smoothly.

Lillian and Gregory had been tracking the dragon and had looped Resnick and the team in on the tracking spell. They'd watched and determined it would be better to allow the dragon to calm. Once the dragon had gone to sleep and reverted to Gryton, they'd waited long enough to determine that it was indeed Gryton in command before landing at a safe distance and approaching on foot.

Erika was still a little out of sorts. She couldn't place why. It wasn't because of Gryton. Though waking up with a naked Hot Stuff and then learning her reaction had been observed was embarrassing enough. But that wasn't it. It was the dreams before that. The ones she couldn't remember.

There'd been a voice...

The voice of the dragon, but she didn't know if it was more than just a dream.

With a headshake, Erika wandered back over to Gryton where he was having a discussion with Gregory while Lillian and Major Resnick relayed everything that had occurred to Command.

She'd learned they were now on the tip of the southern continent instead of its northern shore, where Lord Draydrak's island was only a short distance offshore. But now it would be a long flight back.

Gregory circled his son, studying him. "You should shift back to your dragon form."

Gryton snorted. "Do you want another disaster? Because that is how you will get one."

"If you keep hiding from your dragon nature, it will only grow stronger until it one day has mastery over you."

"That is what I'm trying to stop from happening."

"If you want to maintain control, then you need to learn to both surrender to the dragon and still maintain command over it."

"And how am I supposed to achieve two such polar opposites in the same moment?"

But Erika felt Gryton turning over his father's words. He knew his sire was telling the truth.

"And it will be safer for Erika if you fly her back," Gregory explained. "We flew here on gargoyle back but used a portal spell to cut down the distance. Otherwise, it would have been a three-day flight."

"Then it will be a three-day flight."

"We don't have three days. There is no way the Lady of Battles won't have felt something when the dragon woke. She might not know what has occurred, but she'll know a new power has arisen. She will begin waking her sleeping army and prepare to move upon the Earth."

"Let her have the Earth. The humans are enough of a threat they might even destroy a good chunk of her army, weakening her to give you an easier victory."

"The humans are our allies." The growl that accompanied the words told Erika that Gregory was tiring of his son's negativity.

"Your allies."

"Yours, too. Unless you plan to never see your Null again."

Erika thought Gryton would whoop with delight at that, but he didn't. He glanced over his shoulder to study her. For once she couldn't read him—she noticed she was having trouble with that after he'd shifted back—but he looked unhappy about his father's words.

Could it be he was growing attached to her? And it wasn't just the dragon?

"Fine. I'll tolerate working with the humans on one condition."

"Yes?" His father asked, a look of bemusement on his face.

"You'll kill me if the dragon poses a danger to the Null."

"After what I saw, I'm fairly sure she is safe from the dragon."

"If I agree to continue to aid you, I want you to look into the dragon's mind as you did mine and then do what you must if the beast is too dangerous to allow to live."

Clearly, the big gargoyle was taken aback by his son's words, and Erika could understand why. Gryton was a survivor. Survive at all costs seemed to be his modus operandi. And yet here he was, telling his father to kill him if Gryton lost control and the dragon was too dangerous to allow to live.

"My son, I promise I won't allow you or the dragon to harm our allies. And that you would ask this of me, tells me you have grown a great deal in a short time. That you care for another—the very thing you see as a weakness—will be your strength."

"I doubt that," Gryton muttered to himself as he turned away.

CHAPTER NINE

Gryton

Thinking what he was about to do was folly, but also knowing his father was correct about needing to face the dragon head-on, Gryton stomped over to the Null. What he was about to do didn't affect just him. As strange as it was to dwell on how his actions might affect another, a new part of him knew Erika deserved to know what he was about to do could also affect her adversely.

When he reached her side, he stood looking down at her, trying to figure out what it was about her that the dragon obsessed over, what it was about her that made the great beast so protective and possessive.

Then he decided it was her soul, not the body that housed it, that drew the dragon. Gryton's shoulders slumped as he admitted he found her personality as enchanting as the dragon did. She was fierce and determined and abrasive and smart and strong. But most of all, she was loyal. A trait both he and his dragon admired. And that kind of loyalty deserved honesty from him.

"The dragon is dangerous. My father wants me to embrace him and fly you back to the island. You haven't fed enough to glut your power. If you try to travel through a portal spell, the results might be very unpleasant and very fatal."

"Hmmm. Yeah, I caught that part of the conversation you were having with your father."

"The decision is yours. A longer flight on the back of a gargoyle or I attempt to call forth the dragon."

"I also caught the bit about how we might not get back in time. We can't afford to be late for a fight that might cost us so much if we lose. Call the dragon."

"The dragon is dangerous."

"I know that. But I also know he isn't as dangerous as the deranged demigoddess or the soulless blood witch. This is our destiny, Hot Stuff. Let's go meet it head-on."

"Fine. So shall it be." And just like that he closed his eyes and released the caged beast. The dragon seemed startled at first, but it swiftly got over its surprise and surged forward, up out of the depths of his soul.

"Everyone relax! He's shifting, but not to attack!"

He hoped his Null's words were the truth since he didn't know what kind of mood the volatile creature would be in.

Then the dragon was ripping its way free again, easier this time since he didn't fight it. As soon as the dragon had command, Gryton could feel it overriding his personality. But then it surprised him. Before he'd even put up a fight —and he was planning on fighting for control this time— the dragon was surrendering some of its control back to him.

Or perhaps the dragon was allowing Gryton's consciousness to coexist with it. Whatever the beast's reasoning, they were now merged, and together they trumpeted their claim to the Null at their side.

Claim made, he lowered his head down, his muzzle dipping as his tongue darted out to taste her scent. She was as he remembered. Strength and calmness and steadfastness.

Three traits that soothed him.

While he wanted to scoop her up and fly, to spirit her away from the others around them, he remembered his conversation with his father. It was a battle of sorts to convince the dragon of the merit of his parents' plan to use shadow magic to hide his presence while he made the return journey. At least the dragon was wise enough to see the benefit after Gryton explained.

The Null couldn't yet read the dragon's mind, but she was astute enough to sense the beast's unease at having others work magic upon him. She patted him comfortingly, telling him he needed to wait just a little longer until his sire and dam could weave a glamour around him.

Shadow magic wasn't one of his natural abilities, but he saw the worthiness of their plans and the dragon allowed them to do their work—with a little more soothing from Erika. At last, it was finished, the new power resting like a cool mist against his scales. It wasn't cold enough to be displeasing, and he soon ignored it for Erika was scrambling upon his back.

Then roaring in pleasure and challenge, he summoned his wings. They emerged from his long supple form, bursting out from just behind his shoulders, spreading wide enough to cast the ground behind him in long shadows. Then the shadow magic spread to cover them, and even his own shadow disappeared.

This time, as he prepared to take flight, Erika was nestled just behind his head where his neck merged into his skull. A spikey mane grew from between his horns and parted around his rider, giving her something to hold on to. Gryton admitted it felt surprisingly right to have her there.

Spreading his wings wider, he launched himself off the side of the cliff and sailed out over the ocean, each wing-beat driving him higher into the sky.

His rider issued one startled yelp before she managed to bite it off. He leveled out, cruising at a lower altitude to give her a chance to grow used to flying with him. At first, she clung to him, her body tense with the fear of falling, but soon she started to relax and enjoy the freedom of flight. He dipped playfully several times, and Erika's earlier yelp of fear was replaced with one of delight and laughter.

She shouted for him to go faster, and he did. Joy flowed between them, feeding off each other's emotions. He was soon embracing the joys of sailing through the skies with his Null. He was the king of the sky realm.

Behind them, the others of their supposed escort took to the air and gave chase. With a disdainful snort, he left the Avatars and the other gargoyles with their human riders far behind as he winged his way back toward Lord

Draydrak's temple. If the god of Death thought he was defeated, the other demigod would soon realize his mistake.

The dragon screamed another challenge to the heavens, taunting even the Divine Ones to try and take his Null away and see how much of their beloved creation he destroyed in a plague of fire.

The world could bow before him, or it could burn. The dragon didn't really care which as long as his Null remained with him.

CHAPTER TEN

Erika

Several epiphanies came to her while she was riding on the back of a dragon. First, Erika absolutely loved the freedom of flight. It was the most exhilarating thing she'd ever experienced. Second, she could be both warm and cold at the same time—her legs had been toasty warm thanks to the dragon's generous heat, but her upper body had chilled quickly once they were moving, and at one point she'd feared if she got much colder, her nose might freeze off.

And third, the dragon could be just as much of a cocky bastard as Gryton. She'd found that out when two hours into the flight she'd said she was cold and asked to land on one of the islands forming the archipelago below them.

In response, the dragon had arched his neck and shot

straight up into the air and rolled. When he was at the pinnacle of his arc, gravity had won out over Erika's grip on his spikey mane. She'd screamed as she fell, only to have the sound cut off a moment later when he completed his aerobatics and caught her in his front claws so he could hold her against his chest, his hands sheltering her from the wind.

After she'd had her breath back and her stomach had returned to where it belonged, she'd scolded him for the next half-hour of flight. Eventually, a very sheepish dragon had come in for a landing on one of the islands so she could have a midday meal of some fish he'd snapped out of the ocean for her before they'd continued their journey.

At last, they spotted the rounded peak of the volcanic island where Lord Draydrak had built his temple. As it grew larger, it seemed to rise out of the ocean at the edge of the horizon, and Erika thought it the most beautiful thing she'd seen. She couldn't wait to sit on the hot sand or maybe a sun-warmed rock. She'd had her fill of flight for now.

But dressed appropriately in layers? Oh yeah. She wanted to fly with the dragon again soon.

The dragon came in for a gentle landing, barely jarring her at all. And he was equally gentle as he deposited her on the warm sands. When they'd first approached the island, the beach had been empty, but now she spotted gargoyles flying in their direction.

Beside her, the dragon tensed, his eyes tracking the newcomers as a growl rumbled in his chest.

"Easy. Don't lose your shit. It's likely just an advanced guard unit come to escort us to wherever your parents are waiting."

At least she hoped that was an honor guard and that the Avatars had already arrived and soothed things over with Lord Draydrak. If something had happened to delay them returning by portal spell...

But just then she spotted another group of gargoyles winging down from one of the steep slopes of the extinct volcano. Among them, Erika recognized two female gargoyles. They had to be Anna and Lillian, which likely meant Gregory and Obsidian were part of that group as well.

Erika relaxed and then reached up to give the dragon's scale-covered chest a good scratch. She'd learned he liked that. And as far as she was concerned, a happy dragon was a safer dragon.

Heck, she would sing for the dragon if she thought it would put him in a good mood. But there was no time for a song.

The two groups of gargoyles had nearly reached them by the time a bigger concern came galloping along the beach toward them. This time Lord Draydrak didn't have his swords out.

She took that as a good sign.

The dragon seemed less convinced.

Reaching up, she gave him another good thump. "You're magnificent, and I know you could beat his horse's ass in a fight any day. However, I'm a bit tired after that flight and would love to be able to just sit and chill for a while. No fighting, okay?"

Large dark eyes with flame-ringed irises looked back at her for a moment before homing in on Lord Death again.

"Behave? No more brawling? Please?" She smiled up at the dragon hopefully. "I won't even ask you to shift back to your two-legged form."

Though she really would have liked it if Gryton was in charge when they met with the Avatars and Lord Draydrak, but she figured that would be asking too much.

The two groups of gargoyles and the centaur-like demigod all arrived within seconds of each other. Lord Draydrak spoke first.

"Peace." He raised all four of his hands, showing them empty. "I mean you no harm. I'm sorry for my earlier subterfuge, but I needed to force the dragon out. He will be needed in the coming war. And now there is much I must tell you."

The elemental dragon didn't attack, which was good. Though he didn't relax either. Erika figured that was a start.

CHAPTER ELEVEN

Vaspara

With an affectionate pat to the firedrake's muscular shoulders, Vaspara dismounted. It was a feat she never thought she'd get another chance at, but after she'd been healed, Sorac had asked for an appointment with the Battle Goddess. Once there, she'd learned he'd demanded to be allowed to engage Gryton in the final battle on Earth.

The Battle Goddess was so impressed by the firedrake's rage over what Gryton had done to Vaspara, the goddess had granted him his wish. Once they marched upon that world in the Mortal Realm, Sorac could take out his rage upon the other fire elemental. While Sorac alone likely wouldn't be enough to destabilize Gryton's chaotic power, with the djinn's aid, they would have a much better chance at victory.

The rest of the Battle Goddess's army would work to keep the Avatars busy.

The knowledge that if they won, Sorac would die—there was no way he'd be able to escape fighting in such close quarters with Gryton—pained Vaspara. Her one bit of solace came in the knowledge she would die at his side since the Battle Goddess had decided Sorac would fight longer and harder if Vaspara's life were also over should he fail.

So, she would fly to war on the back of her beloved firedrake, and they would die together as she'd always imagined their ending. As for their draklings, the Goddess had instructed the djinn to store more than enough of his power in dozens of ward-stone containers so if the djinn was dragged back to the Spirit Realm by the Avatars during the war, there would be enough compatible magic in storage to feed the little ones until they were weaned and able to fend for themselves.

It wasn't how Vaspara would have wanted things to end, but at least if they won this war, Sorac's young would have a chance to grow up. That was all she could really ask for. After all, the Lady of Battles was showing great benevolence by allowing Vaspara the opportunity to die with Sorac.

And before that end, she and Sorac were to be granted some leniency. Like today, they were allowed to travel together with the other captains to the valley network where the stone sleepers were stored under layers of magical protections.

The Lady of Battles knew of the logistical problems of having such a vast standing army. It required enormous amounts of resources, more than what could be easily sustained, so in order to overcome that problem, she'd come up with the idea of enchanting two-thirds of her army until they were needed.

Vaspara admitted it also had another benefit. The most savage and unruly of the army could be enchanted to sleep like stone statues, effectively resulting in a way to keep the peace with as little effort as possible. As each new generation was trained up until they were masters in the art of combat, they were either enchanted to sleep until they were needed or were held back to complete the next level to become officers.

But war was upon them, and there was no more time for training, which was why she and Sorac and all the rest of the captains had been dispatched to this place today.

Tilting her head to glance up at Sorac, she leaned forward and then rested a hand on his right foreleg.

"Thank you. As always, it's much quicker to fly than ride out here."

He dipped his broad muzzle and breathed in her scent. "It is always a pleasure to fly through the skies with you on my back."

A rare smile touched her lips but soon vanished.

While she had shown much leniency, the Lady of Battles hadn't forgiven them. They were both still wrapped in layers of the djinn and the blood witch's magic. Sorac was forced to remain in his firedrake form, forbidden to shift back. The longer he remained in his true form, the harder it would be for him to change back to his two-legged shape. If he stayed in his drake form long enough, he'd lose the ability to shift to a man.

The time they made love when he was healing her a few days before might be the last time they ever made love again. Vaspara wasn't looking forward to having to feed on another male to keep her strength up, but she hoped if they both behaved and proved they were the most skilled and respected of the captains—not counting Bervicta— then she hoped the Battle Goddess would relax that restriction and allow Sorac to resume the form of a man upon occasion.

But today they needed to wake their battalions and show them to be the most disciplined and most highly skilled of all the army. They also had another motive for coming more swiftly than the other captains. In the center of the valley, between her and Sorac's battalions was another group of elite warriors.

They were Commander Gryton's special pupils. He'd always had contingency plans, which was why he was such a good commander. These males and females were trained in the art of command and were intended to act as a secondary leadership for the army if their enemies somehow managed to take out the primary leadership at some point in a future war.

The Lady of Battles hadn't ordered they be awakened, but Vaspara thought that was likely because she didn't know Gryton had segregated them from the regular battalions and kept them tucked here in this valley between her and Sorac's forces.

"Should we awaken our own battalions first and get

them up to speed on everything that has happened? Or wake the Elite?"

"Let's wake our own first," Vaspara said with a hint of unease. "We'll see how that goes."

He nodded but remained silent, and she imagined he was thinking the same thing.

Part of the waking process required that they share their memories with the sleeping battalion members. Always before she'd shared all her accomplishments with a bit of pride. It let the battalion know she was still a fierce and skilled warrior, worthy of leading them into battle and dying beside them if that was required. But now they would see that she'd turned her back on her goddess and convinced the big firedrake to come with her. They would know about the draklings and that she loved them and their father more than her Goddess.

Many would see that as treason and weakness.

"They will probably seek to depose me, and rightly so." She paused as she looked at the firedrake. "You must allow them to do that if that is their wish. It is their right. A battalion must have a strong leader they can believe in. Otherwise, there is the risk of everything falling apart on the battlefield."

Sorac growled menacingly, but after a moment he nodded his agreement. "I will not let them harm you, though.

"I do not believe you need to worry about that. They will see that I am valuable as a way to control you."

"I will still stand beside you, my beloved," Sorac hissed, his lips pulling back from his teeth. "And make sure they see *all* that has been going on. How the Battle Goddess has allowed a blood witch far too much leniency. How we had to steal away our own servants to save them. How even Gryton has abandoned the Lady of Battles."

Ice suddenly ran through her veins. "Sorac, no! Do nothing to incite a civil war. That way leads to all our deaths."

He huffed softly. "Fine. But I won't hide the truth from them. I'll let them see everything and decide for themselves. And if one or more of them decide to dispose of the blood witch and the djinn, so be it."

"No. We need to keep the djinn around until he has stored up enough of his power that if something happens to us, our draklings won't starve."

The big drake nodded once and then he bowed his head close to hers. "I wish there was a future where we could have lived out our days in peace, raising our little ones and watching them grow and have little hatchlings of their own."

She gave him a sad smile. "Gryton once told me your mother believed there were many realms existing side by side, and that in some of them there would be other Vasparas and Soracs and Grytons and Bervictas. If she was correct, then maybe in some other realm or world or time, there is a place where we didn't take the djinn when we escaped with your eggs, and we are even now raising them, living and loving and free."

Sorac was silent for a time. When he at last blinked and focused on her, he nuzzled her gently. "I like that thought, my beloved."

"Come then. Let's go. We might not have a happy

ending in our future, but we can at least comport ourselves with honor and integrity."

"Honor and integrity are in short supply it seems," he rumbled out. "After all, the Lady of Battles betrayed all of us a very long time ago by allowing a soul feeder among our ranks."

"That might be true. But keep that thought to yourself, you great lizard. I don't want to see you die before you must."

"Fair enough."

Together they made their way down the valley's northern slope. It was a naturally broad valley, more like a canyon system, but over thousands of years, they'd expanded the area at key points to make room for the ever-growing army. Even walking swiftly, the march was long, and morning soon turned into afternoon.

They reached the midpoint of her battalions' location and stopped at a natural rise sticking out of the otherwise gentle slope. Below her, the incline led down to where the sleeping army waited in the carefully arranged terraces.

"This is as good as any spot," Vaspara muttered as she climbed the side of the natural ledge.

Sorac remained below her, his haunches on the ground, tail curled around his legs, head held high and proud as he stood next to her.

"You could at least look humble about our failings."

"There is nothing to be humble about. I certainly don't view your love as a weakness to be hidden away so others don't see it," he said in a rumbling purr. "Let them look upon us. We are still fierce and masters of ourselves. And we were loyal to the Battle Goddess for as long as possible.

It was the blood witch who convinced the Battle Goddess to send us to watch over that suicide mission into gargoyle territory, all so Taryin could experiment with her twisted foul magics."

"Your prejudice is showing again, my love."

The drake snorted. "It's not prejudiced if I'm telling the facts as they unfolded."

"Still, I would suggest you allow your battalion to see the facts without your emotions painting them in a particular color."

"Fine. You have my word I'll let them all see what a disaster the blood witch will bring upon them for themselves."

"That's a better idea." She flashed him a grin and then closed her eyes and centered herself. Turning her hands palm up, she spread them wide and began chanting the words of the spell even as her magic rose to answer her call. At the first touch of her power, the layers of protection covering the valley flared to life, becoming visible to the naked eye.

Soon she was mentally wading deep into the spell and manipulating the command nodes, signaling them to begin waking the sleepers. The new commands slowly spread out over the entire netting, making it shimmer brighter as it turned from a pale blue to a sparkling emerald-hue.

Once the new commands reached the distant outer edge of the spell net, the entire construction shivered once and then began to descend over the waiting statues. The ones nearer to her and Sorac's location were the first the spell touched, and their stone-like skin gave way to flesh and blood bodies. Slowly the spell net dipped lower into the valley, continuing to reach new rows of statues, waking them as it had the first.

As the spell continued its work, she studied the first line of warriors spread out in either direction, checking to see that they all returned to life and none of them were in severe distress.

She'd performed the waking five times before and knew it was never an easy spell to rouse from. Her battalion would all need three or four days to feed and fully recover, but so far, all in her line of sight were doing well enough.

"They are strong," Sorac said with a little pride.

"Of course they are. When have I ever allowed weakness to take root in any of my warriors?"

Sorac chuckled. "Point taken. I would expect nothing less from the soldiers under mighty Vaspara's command. After all, she was second only to Commander Gryton and me."

"You're getting cocky, lizardman. It was the other way around as I remember it. You were second only to Commander Gryton and me."

The firedrake snorted. "I must be getting confused between battle sport and bed sport, and the way I make you whine and moan and scream when you're under me."

Vaspara snorted. "I was allowing you to retain your sense of masculinity. If we ever get the chance to play at bed sports again, I'll strip you of your delusions, and it will be you moaning and crying and begging while I work my mastery over that impressive cock of yours, mighty firedrake."

"I love it when you talk dirty, my succubus. And while I would love to discover where this will lead," he grinned at her, his teeth gleaming in the sun, "your battalion will soon need your guidance."

He was correct. Closing her eyes again, she triggered the second part of the spell. This was far less showy but required much more concentration. Calling up the most important memories of the last year, she began to weave the spell that would deliver each memory into the minds of the soldiers under her command. She started with the defection of River and how she'd escaped to the Mortal Realm with her mate and her son to join the Avatars.

Once that memory was racing down the lines of the spell net, she next showed how Gryton had gone in pursuit of River, and as a result of that, other members of the Battle Goddess's army had managed to recapture River's son. Later another opportunity had presented itself in the form of the cub's new Kyrsu coming after him.

Vaspara showed how swiftly the two had excelled in their training, and how they were greater assets than River and Stalks the Darkness. She gave the soldiers a moment to assimilate what they'd just learned. Once she was confident they were ready for the next, she showed that how unknown to Vaspara and everyone else, while Gryton had been in the Mortal Realm, he'd encountered the Mother's Sorceress and had flipped sides, only returning to the Magic Realm to act as a spy and to attempt to rescue the cub.

There was a great stirring in the ranks at this news, but they were too well trained to speak out yet, and she focused on the next bit of news. Blood Witch Taryin had acted against orders and attempted to weave one of her slave spells upon Anna and Shadowlight, but the two rebelled, unwilling to be slaves to such a dark spell. They managed to inflict what would have been a mortal wound upon the witch, but in their youth and inexperience, they'd left her locked in a cage with Captains Ninara and Honnan instead of finishing her off. The witch fed upon the two captains, devouring their lifeforce and then their souls to regenerate herself.

Gryton had then fought the witch and the other remaining captains to allow Anna and Shadowlight the time they needed to escape to Lord Death. Faced with impossible odds, Gryton was eventually overcome, and the Battle Goddess tortured him.

The Lady of Battles had planned to set his power cascading out of control and then toss him through a portal spell linked to the world in the Mortal Realm where the Avatars resided. If all had gone as planned, Gryton would have died, rising into a fiery sun. But the Avatars had infiltrated the Goddess's kingdom in secret and rescued their son, killing a great many of the Battle Goddess's warriors in the process.

Vaspara paused to allow her warriors to assimilate everything she'd just fed them. Once she deemed them ready for the rest, she continued to tell of how the captains' numbers had been cut in half from the previous events.

But the witch had survived and soon began creating new spells to hunt and track Shadowlight and Anna. When she discovered she couldn't achieve her plans using a blood witch's magic—a gargoyle would scent that stink and hunt it out—she summoned a djinn.

This news caused another great stirring among the

warriors spread out in the valley below. It wasn't as great as the news about Gryton being the Avatars son, but a djinn was dreadfully dangerous.

While the memory of how the blood witch began hunting and feeding on the servants—some loyal families having served for generations—might not be strictly needed for the soldiers to do their duties, Vaspara decided to show them the witch's callousness anyway.

Then she showed how Sorac had acted to save his and Vaspara's servants by secreting them away to protect those loyal servants.

It set the tone for the next part, of how the Battle Goddess had sent a small force led by the newest captain into gargoyle territory to deliver the spell the witch and the djinn had come up with to locate and return Anna and Shadowlight to the Lady of Battles.

Vaspara and Sorac were sent to oversee the new captain, but they were not in command of the ill-fated venture. Somehow the gargoyles discovered the tracking spells and set their own trap. A trap the young captain led the small company into. It was a blood bath, everyone besides Vaspara and Sorac being slaughtered by the gargoyles.

Vaspara showed that only her talent with a sword and Sorac's might had allowed them to capture two of the Legion warriors and use them to bargain for their own escape. She didn't hesitate to show them how betrayed and used she'd felt knowing the Lady of Battles would allow the blood witch to do whatever she wished to achieve an end.

Then after she'd swallowed that bit of bitter reality, she had come to realize everyone back home would think they were dead. She'd convinced Sorac they could just disappear, join their servants and start a new life elsewhere. Besides, he had a nest with fourteen eggs hidden away, and if servants weren't safe, what guarantee did he have that the witch wouldn't eventually turn her attention to them?

Vaspara implied she'd seduced the big firedrake into going along with her plan to save his young.

"Hah. And there goes the succubus trying to protect me again," Sorac rumbled, his words carrying far and wide. "I've loved Vaspara for centuries and have always wanted to start a life with her, but there was one problem. I couldn't leave my clutch vulnerable to Blood Witch Taryin." The big drake lowered his muzzle so he could affectionately nuzzle her.

"*Sorac,*" she sent along a private link, "*I don't think it was a good idea to show them how much you care about me.*"

"*I am done with deceit. Let them see our devotion to each other. They are smart enough to know our love has always been a strength, not a weakness.*"

Aloud, he continued. "Vaspara aided me in going back to collect my clutch in secret. Unbeknownst to us, the djinn had sensed our return and was waiting for us. He demanded we liberate his bottle and escape with him. In exchange for our aid, he would allow us to take my eggs from that place. We did as he asked."

Vaspara then showed the newly awakened battalion the rest. She even allowed them to glimpse her awe and terror the day she'd been at the nest when the first egg began to hatch and later her poor attempts at being a mother. But as much as she'd feared to be a mother, the little ones had won her heart, and she would do anything to see them safe.

Then the day came where Blood Witch Taryin and Captain Bervicta arrived on the island and captured the little ones. She and Sorac had surrendered to protect the hatchlings, and now they were slaves to the blood witch.

Vaspara looked out over the valley, making eye contact with as many of her soldiers as she could. "Do not make the same mistake we did. Do not toss away your honor and respect, everything you've worked for, in a moment of weakness. The Lady of Battles was merciful to us because of all the years of service we performed for her. She will not be so merciful a second time."

"Merciful is not the word I would have used to describe what she has allowed the witch to do to us." The firedrake's thoughts were accompanied by a huff.

"I know. And the battalion is smart enough to know that I am warning them of what they have to look forward to."

"There is that."

Vaspara nodded to the firedrake and then turned her gaze back out to the valley and the soldiers waiting there.

"While the Lady of Battles may have restored our titles and ability to command, she will not strike out if any of you are not confident in my ability to lead and wish to challenge me for leadership." Vaspara stepped away from Sorac and held her arms out wide. "Come. Speak now and I will answer your challenge in three days, once you are recovered."

At last, the murmuring of voices rolled across the valley. Soldiers cast subtle glances to their left and right as if seeking guidance from their neighbor.

"They are conflicted. We clearly betrayed our duties, and yet

they aren't certain our choices weren't forced by the leniency the Battle Goddess has given her dark witch."

"Yes. But will it be enough?"

"We shall see." Sorac sat with his tail curled around his haunches, the tip flicking gently. He looked bored, but she sensed the tension in his body, the willingness to strike if anyone threatened Vaspara outside of a formal challenge.

At last, the battalion grew quiet once more, and a few individuals moved through the throng and organized into a line directly in front of where she and Sorac stood. Vaspara kept a neutral expression on her face while she awaited their verdict.

Of the twenty lined up before them, three stepped forward to act as spokespersons for the rest of the battalion. She recognized each of them. After all, she'd trained them, spending extra time with the most skilled of her students.

Brunin, a blond-haired incubus who also had the distinction of being one of her cousins, was the first to speak. "If the Lady of Battles is content that you remain her captain, I am equally content to continue to call you my captain as well."

He bowed deeply before stepping back into his place in line. Vernik, a male of centaur blood approached next. He too bowed deeply. "I have no issue calling one of the most beautiful women in the army my leader."

Sorac gave a growling laugh at the centaur's words. "As long as all you do is look, stallion. She's my mate now."

Vaspara smacked Sorac on the muzzle. *"Not helping, Lizardman."*

"So far, so good. We'll have to see about the last one." He just grinned as the third person approached.

The female of mixed harpy-sidhe blood was tall and solidly built, with both a set of wings and arms like Bervicta. Though she lacked the harpy captain's height, nor was she quite as broad in the shoulders and chest. But that didn't mean Saskurna wasn't deadly in her own right. She was a superb assassin. It was said she could even sneak up on a gargoyle and give the surprised male a good grope before burying her blade in his body.

Vaspara secretly thought that might just be an exaggerated rumor. Gargoyles were notoriously hard to approach in secret. Though she wouldn't put it past a harpy to attempt to feel up a gargoyle if given a chance. They were bold females that generally took what they wanted.

If any of the soldiers under Vaspara's command were to issue a challenge, she'd expect it of this female. But Saskurna surprised her by dipping into a deep bow and then straightening.

"What those two lovely males weren't masculine enough to admit is that no one wants to take you on in a battle for leadership." The female shrugged her wings. "Perhaps if the current climate were different someone would desire the power enough to risk their neck, but with a blood witch slinking around, devouring unsuspecting souls, no one wants the distinction of becoming a new captain and drawing the witch or the djinn's attention. Doesn't sound very good for one's long-term survival."

"I detect no lies," Sorac offered.

Vaspara agreed. She'd detected no deceit in any of the soldiers.

"Very well. Ready yourselves to return to the city. The other members of our battalion are already setting up tents in the valley below the city."

The battalion came to attention, and the loud thump of many fists hitting breastplates in a salute rang across the valley. She repeated the motion in answer. Next she turned to Sorac and nodded her head.

He dipped his head low enough she could easily mount, and then they were winging their way farther down the valley to Sorac's sleeping battalion. Once they reached them, Sorac did as Vaspara had done before him and soon his soldiers were awake and hearing the same tale from Sorac's lips.

They responded in much the same manner as hers had. Though they were swifter to confirm no one wanted to challenge the firedrake's leadership. While Sorac was giving his men their orders to return to the city to begin gathering supplies, Bervicta came winging her way into the valley.

"Male, you fly entirely too fast. How is your leader supposed to keep up?" But Bervicta's voice was humorous. Her eyes darted over the sea of bodies already starting to march down the valley on their way to the fortress city. "It went well, I take it?"

"Yes, surprisingly."

"Not so much of a surprise to me. No one ever enjoys meeting you in the ring even when it's just for practice. A fight that might end in death with an angry firedrake looking on?" She snorted. "No. I'm not surprised you didn't get a challenger."

"Sorac in firedrake form does make a very menacing partner."

"Exactly. By the way, did you wish to stay and watch me awaken Gryton's Elites?" Bervicta grinned. "It certainly won't hurt if a firedrake is standing on my one side, steam rolling out his mouth while you stand at the other shoulder glowering that look of yours that can make a male's cock both hard and want to crawl between his own legs to hide at the same time."

Vaspara laughed at the harpy's words and accompanying gestures. "I will stand at your side."

"Good, because I was going to command you both if you didn't agree." She glanced at the stone soldiers still lined up in formations. "If anyone is willing to offer a challenge to yours, mine, or Sorac's leadership, it will be one of Gryton's personal pets."

But even those soldiers didn't offer a challenge upon waking and learning all that had transpired since the last time they'd been awake. Though they did surprise Vaspara by deciding to split themselves among the twelve other battalions instead of forming a thirteenth.

Once their battalions were moving, Vaspara, Sorac, and Bervicta began the flight back home.

"The Elites are up to something," Bervicta hissed from her position behind Vaspara on Sorac's back. The drake had offered to fly the harpy back to the fortress so they could all have everything ready for their newly awakened soldiers' return.

"Yes," Sorac agreed in a rumble.

"You mean how they split themselves up so they will have spies in all the other battalions?" Vaspara knew what she said was true. "They came to that consensus too swiftly for it to be anything other than a contingency Gryton put into place in case of his absence."

"But that assumes they still trust him after his betrayal," the harpy said, sounding highly doubtful of the idea that the soldiers would still trust in anything Gryton put into motion.

"His betrayal doesn't negate his intellect and skills as a tactician. While Gryton's defection has forced his Elites to sever all ties of loyalty to him, that in no way means they are no longer loyal to each other. I think they plan to measure the other command-level officers in order to determine who all they need to defeat to take control of each battalion."

Bervicta swore. "Well, that's auspicious. And if they're successful, the Battle Goddess will admire the boldness of such a plan and likely let them live to command her army. If we don't wish to be a part of the captains who are overthrown, I suggest we all start working with the Elites to earn their trust and loyalty.

CHAPTER TWELVE

Erika

Lord Death's island home was a tropical paradise. Erika hadn't had time to see much of it the first time. But now that she'd had a chance for a brief look around, she admitted she wouldn't mind spending some leave time in a place like this.

Heck, tourists would have paid hundreds of dollars for a week here. Well, if not for the host being death incarnate and all that.

Presently, she and her new dragon friend—Gryton still hadn't shifted back—were seated off to one side of a natural amphitheater. Benches lined three of the surrounding slopes with the fourth side being open to the ocean.

The place was packed with gargoyles and dryads. If she

was to guess, the entire population of the island had turned out. Though there was an invisible two-hundred-foot bubble around the dragon that everyone treated with a healthy respect. And the dragon was free with his hissing reminders when a gargoyle or dryad approached too closely.

Only Lillian and Gregory tested the dragon by crossing that invisible line and approaching Erika.

"Are you well?" Lillian asked her, even as the woman's gaze cut away to track the slightest shift in the dragon's body.

"Yes. Surprisingly well. Though my power doesn't seem to be feeding on the dragon's fire magic. I don't know why. And he can't or won't talk."

The Sorceress looked thoughtful for a moment. "I think I know why. He's in control of his power far better than Gryton ever was, and your ability knows it and doesn't consider him a danger, at least not to himself." She paused and looked up at the dragon. "I mean no insult, my son. But it seems that now that your dragon has matured, your fire magic is no longer at war with you. I think all this time your dragon has been battling to assume your natural form."

The dragon just tilted his head to study Lillian. After a moment, he rumbled something and nuzzled his mother. When his father ventured closer, Gregory was rewarded with a soft growl.

The gargoyle scowled up at the dragon. "Watch your tongue, pup. You are still a long way from being my match, but if you remain civil, I'll teach you all I know about mastery over the powers of the universe and your own mind."

Snorting softly, the dragon nodded infinitesimally and then settled down to wait. As usual, his tail curled around Erika, dragging her closer.

"Is he ever going to get less..." She was going to say needy but thought better of that. "Less...tactile?"

Lillian looked mildly concerned, but Gregory just laughed. "Not likely. Or at least not any time soon. He's finally found someone he trusts enough to lavish affection on."

"I have to agree with my mate," Lillian said. "Gryton in his dragon form is a little like a dog with a favorite toy."

"Heck, as long as he's not raging, I'm cool with being his dog toy." She looked up at his generous teeth. "As long as I'm not his chew toy, all's good."

Lillian nodded at the dragon. "We'll still keep a close eye on his mental state, but for now I think he is calm enough to sit while Lord Draydrak tells us what he knows about Gregory's and my last life together."

Erika nodded and looked around at all the gargoyles arriving. The sky was still black with wings as more of the island's residents came in for landings among the bench-lined slopes. Something else occurred to her.

"Is Lord Draydrak just going to divulge state secrets in front of everyone?"

Lillian chuckled. "Things are different here. Until Haven, which has now been explained to everyone, there were no secrets among the Legion members. Well, there are little secrets, of course. But if something affects every-one, then everyone has the right to know about it. Besides, gargoyles are some of the worse gossips. No secret would long survive here. I'm amazed Haven managed to remain covert. I suppose the credit must go to Draydrak for not allowing that knowledge to escape."

Erika turned to look where the demigod in question was striding up the slope facing the ocean. When he approached the Avatars and the dragon, he held his hands out to show them empty as he had the last time.

"I am glad you have agreed to stay and listen," he told the dragon. "We must put our differences aside and learn to work together to have any chance of winning the coming war."

After he said his piece, Lord Draydrak backed away, giving them a little space. Which was good because the dragon wasn't overly happy at Lord Death's nearness.

She patted the dragon's closest foreleg more to reassure herself than him. While Adept Thayn was calling the assembly to order, Erika glanced up at the dragon. "You really do need a name."

His muzzle dipped lower, and he huffed softly once more.

"I also wish I knew what that meant." She shrugged. "I suppose if you don't tell me your name, I'll just have to come up with one on my own. Contingent on if you like it, of course."

The dragon rumbled but only lowered his head to rest on his forearms.

But the naming of her new dragon mount would have to wait. Adept Thayn was finished and bowing toward Lord Draydrak. The demigod nodded.

"We are here today because of a plan set in motion over

six thousand years ago, during the last time the Avatars ventured outside of the Spirit Realm. That last life ended when they created the elemental dragon sitting here with us today." Draydrak's voice took on a storytelling quality. "The Divine Ones had planned to use the Avatars, in their last lifetime, to bring back the healed Shieldbearer."

That revelation got a mutter of surprise from the audience. Even the Avatars looked surprised by the news, but Draydrak merely continued.

"It wasn't until after I destroyed the Shieldbearer and sent him back to the Divine Ones for healing that I discovered the source of his corruption. He'd gone to battle a true demon escaped from the void. The Shieldbearer was still young and wished to prove himself to his mate. But it was foolish to go after a demon of the void by himself. Even my twin and I wouldn't face one of those beasts without several gargoyles or a djinn."

Erika wondered what set demons of the void apart from the Battle Goddess's army and other nasty things that went bump in the night.

"But the demon was cunning even in defeat," Lord Draydrak continued. "While the Shieldbearer had won the battle and destroyed the demon, it had still whispered seductive lies into his mind as it died, whispering that my twin preferred me to battle at her side, that I was a fiercer, more skilled warrior. And in her secret heart, she wished I wasn't her brother at all, but instead her mate."

Wow. Someone had nerves of steel and wasn't easily embarrassed, Erika reflected. And he'd said that all without flinching.

"None of it was true, but the demon's words festered in

the Shieldbearer's heart until slowly, over time, his jealousy grew. Then one day he decided if he could beat me and steal my powers, he'd also steal my place in the Battle Goddess's heart. He believed she would then see he was her perfect mate."

Draydrak sighed. "Of course, the Shieldbearer was already my sister's entire world. From the moment the Avatars had come together by Divine edict and birthed the Shieldbearer into the Universe, my twin loved him without hesitation. He completed her soul."

Draydrak glanced down upon the fae, gargoyles, and humans gathered around. Perhaps taking pity on them, he folded his legs under him and sat. They would still have to crane their necks, but Erika appreciated the gesture.

A moment later the big dragon changed positions as well, settling to sit on his haunches in a more upright position while he cradled Erika in his hands. Suddenly she didn't have to crane her neck to study Draydrak.

She patted the dragon's warm palm. "Thanks, big guy."

The dragon made a soft huffing sound and a jet of steam issued from between his teeth.

Off on the other side of the amphitheater, Draydrak flicked his wings and folded them tight to his back. Comfortable at last, he continued his tale.

"It wasn't until after I'd sent the Shieldbearer back to the Spirit Realm to be purified and healed that I realized the full extent of what his loss would do to my twin. I foolishly thought I could make her understand, that my love for my twin would be enough to help her deal with her grief until the Shieldbearer was healed and reborn to walk the universe with her once more."

He paused again, one hoof pawing at the sand floor of the arena before he noticed the action and stopped. "But one thing I hadn't foreseen was that the Shieldbearer would need a great deal of healing to purify his spirit and that the Divine Ones wouldn't let anyone see him during that time."

Draydrak closed his eyes for a moment, but the depth of his regret was still evident in his body language. "My Twin's rage spiraled into insanity, and that madness destroyed worlds."

"It was not your fault," Gregory said softly. "None of it was."

"Yes. I know my actions were necessary, but I realized too late what it would cost the three realms. I doubted myself after that," he admitted. "I began to think that perhaps I should have gone to my Twin first and told her what I'd found and then together we could deal with the Shieldbearer. That way it would be my blow that ended his life, but my twin would have been there with him to hold him until his power unraveled and his soul was ready to journey back to the Spirit Realm where he could heal. I think my twin would have gone with him peacefully if events had unfolded that way."

A snorting sound of dissension came from within the largest group of gargoyles gathered along the southern side of the arena. A moment later, a gargoyle was leaping up onto Lord Draydrak's foreleg.

"The Battle Goddess would never have done what needed to be done," the gargoyle challenged, and Erika recognized Thayn's voice. "And I wouldn't bet that she wasn't corrupted by her mate after his run-in with the void demon. Old friend, you did the only thing you could to protect the three realms."

"Perhaps," the Lord of the Underworld agreed. Then, his gaze turning to where Erika sat upon the dragon's palm, he continued. "In the Avatars' last mortal lifetime, the Divine Ones had intended to use them to rebirth the Shieldbearer in the hope he would be able to persuade his mate to surrender her power and return to the Spirit Realm to be healed by the Divine Ones as he had been."

Thayn snorted again.

Draydrak faced the elder, but he spoke to everyone as he continued. "As you can imagine from Thayn's response, like him, not all the great players agreed upon this path. Many of the djinns believed, like Thayn did, that such a path would just put the Shieldbearer at risk of being corrupted once more, by the Battle Goddess this time. If he had indeed passed a taint to his mate, then she could just as easily give the infection back to him."

Erika couldn't help but think a particular group of immortals needed a health class to learn about safe sex. She'd only just finished that thought when Lord Draydrak looked back at her, and she had the distinct impression he was silently laughing.

Shit? Could he read thoughts? Of course he could.

"Yes, Null," came a rich, mellow voice directly into her head. *"One of my gifts is to touch the minds of all creatures, so that I may soothe them at the moment of their death. But the gift comes in handy for other things, too."*

"Ah. Sorry, I'll try to keep my thoughts more respectful," she hedged, not knowing what else to promise a demigod.

"No need, ancient one. I have heard and seen many things in my long lifetime, and I am not easily offended."

While it was good he wasn't easily offended, she was having trouble with everyone randomly addressing her as old soul or ancient one or some such. But Lord Death didn't seem concerned with her worries and continued with his tale.

"It wasn't the first time, and likely won't be the last, that the djinns have bickered amongst themselves over one of the Divine Ones' plans. What made this time different was that the Avatar was uncertain of the wisdom of reuniting the Lady of Battles with her Shieldbearer."

Erika noticed a not-so-subtle shift in Gregory's posture. This was news to him. Actually, the entire tale was probably new to the pair. After all, they claimed to have no memory of their last lifetime together that resulted in Gryton's birth.

"Then once the Avatar sundered its soul to be reborn as the Gargoyle Protector and the Mother's Sorceress, they became even more certain of the risk of their creator's plan. In the end, they sided with the oldest of the djinns. While the Sorceress would have agreed to wait and first carry out the Divine Ones' plan before trying her own, she was swayed by her Gargoyle Protector and the eldest of the djinns. Together the three of them concocted a plan to fight the Lady of Battles and finally send her back to the Divine Ones for healing."

"I was at odds with my Sorceress?" Gregory sounded positively doubtful of the validity of the news.

"For a very short time, yes, you believed in something enough to act against your other half."

"It wasn't just him," Thayn piped up. "Both legions' councils also believed something more direct was needed to deal with the Battle Goddess."

Lord Death nodded. "Yes. You wished to find a way to kill my Twin."

"You know it needs to be done. She'll never surrender, not even to the Shieldbearer."

Draydrak looked off into the distance, his body still. If he breathed, Erika couldn't see it. Perhaps he didn't need to breathe and just did sometimes to put other people at ease? After a long silence, Draydrak stirred, his wings shifting slightly.

"And so, it came to be that the Avatars birthed their son into the universe, imbibing him with power as great as, or perhaps greater than, what my twin and I command. An elemental dragon rose out of the destruction of the Avatars' mortal bodies. The backlash of magic was even greater than they'd expected, and their soul was damaged by Gryton's birth. They weren't able to impart their memories to him. His true purpose was lost to him."

Draydrak turned his attention to Lillian and Gregory. "Had you confided in me before you acted, I would have been able to aid you, protected you against the ravages of your own power as you gave too much of yourselves to your son. But by the time I sensed what you were doing, it was too late, and you were too far away to help. I couldn't leave my temple without also freeing my Twin from the duality curse."

Gregory paced in front of Lord Draydrak. "I remember none of this," he admitted. "The few memories Gryton did manage to absorb before my Sorceress and I returned to the Spirit Realm were too chaotic to decipher."

"Yet it happened, and it nearly destroyed the Avatar soul as well. Only with the aid of the oldest djinn, were you able to reunite your shattered soul in the Spirit Realm. Only cocooned in his power, his essence wrapped around you like a shield, were you able to heal and restore your soul to what it had been before your last lifetime and Gryton's birth."

Gregory stilled; his tail frozen in mid-swing. While Erika wasn't completely familiar with gargoyle body language, she was starting to catch a few things. And every inch of the gargoyle spoke of his shock.

"I did not understand how or why it had come about, but in this lifetime, I have felt less," Gregory uttered.

"Yes," Lord Death agreed. "In time, you and your other half will be fully restored. But in this lifetime, you both are still suffering the effects of what Gryton's birth did to your soul. My twin knew this. That is how she managed to trap the female half of your soul and forced her to be born into a vessel of the Battle Goddess's choosing."

Gregory nodded sharply. "I have wondered how your twin managed such a thing."

"But you overcame my sister's plans. Even Gryton has escaped her." Lord Draydrak turned to face the dragon, something he seemed to avoid, likely knowing it triggered aggression in the dragon. But this time Death met the fire elemental's gaze. "My intent was not to kill you. I had sent my gargoyles to capture you and bring you back here where I could study you and determine if what the Avatars had birthed into the universe was friend or foe."

The dragon hissed a warning, his lips pulling back as fire licked between his teeth.

"Easy. I have since seen enough of how you protected the Null to know you are capable of caring for something other than yourself. A servant of the void cares for no one. You might have issues you need to work through, to master control over your chaotic nature, but if you so choose, you can be a worthy servant of the light."

The dragon sneered. Erika had no other word for the expression on the dragon's face in the moments before he lowered his head threateningly at Draydrak and closed his talon-tipped fingers around her and brought her closer to his chest.

Lord Death held his hands out, palms up once more. "Or, if you wish, you do not have to serve at all. As long as you do no more evil, the Divine Ones will let you go unmolested. Though like all beings, you will one day stand before them and be judged."

The dragon didn't relax, but he didn't growl either, so Erika took that as a good sign.

Draydrak tilted his head and studied Erika for a moment before his gaze lifted back to the dragon. "Though the Null will join our fight. I can see that much. It is in her nature. And if you care for the Null as much as I think you do, you will fight beside her. She'll certainly have a better chance of surviving the coming war with you as a partner, rather than alone."

"I will fight alongside my Null and destroy whatever enemies she wishes me to annihilate." The dragon's voice was deep and rich and somehow held a hint of a roaring fire to it. The tone made Erika's ears vibrate. "But I serve no others. Not you. Not the Avatars. Not even your Divine Ones."

A glance around showed everyone else was as surprised by the dragon's words as Erika was.

Lord Draydrak drew back a few more steps and then bowed to the dragon. "Your aid is welcome. After the war is over, you will be free to go anywhere you wish, and no one will come after you as long as you never harm innocents."

The dragon rumbled something that sounded like a vicious sort of humor, but then he turned his back on Lord Death, and Erika was no longer caged by his claws. Instead she now sat on his hand. Above her, all she could see was his long narrow muzzle where it flared out into what would have been his cheeks in a human. The elegant feelers waved softly in the breeze.

Two beautiful solid dark eyes with flames deep in their centers stared back at her. *"I am yours,"* the dragon whispered. *"I shall serve only you."*

Erika licked her lips nervously. "Okay."

His warm breath washed over her. *"And you are equally mine and will serve only me."*

Oh boy. Her superiors were going to have some words about that. But she wasn't stupid enough to challenge the elemental dragon. He was far too volatile. Gryton needed more time to learn to control this side of his nature.

Squaring her shoulders, Erika reached out and gave his sizeable clawed thumb a reassuring pat. "Let's start with the war that's coming, and we'll decide where and what to do from there? In the meantime, I'm more than happy to have you as my friend and partner." She grinned suddenly. "A girl couldn't ask for a more splendid partner."

The dragon puffed up his chest and preened at her compliment.

Lord Draydrak laughed. "The two of you will be the Light's battering ram. Together you will help us defeat the blood witch and extract the oldest of the djinn from her clutches while the Avatars and I deal with my sister."

Then the god of death turned from them to address the Avatars and the rest of the assembly.

Erika was just thinking it might be smoother sailing from then on.

At least that's what she'd hoped until Lord Draydrak drew himself up to his full height once more, his earlier openness and friendliness falling away.

"There is just one other issue we must address here today."

The stadium-like structure went absolutely silent. No small feat for an area that was packed body to body with a good ten thousand gargoyles and dryads.

Something must have passed between demigod and dragon for the fire elemental drew Erika closer to his chest and took a step toward the cliff and open sky.

"Hey! Where are you going?" She smacked his thumb repeatedly to get his attention. "We can't just leave. What's going on?"

"A fight to determine which pair of Avatars will lead. I will take you to a safe distance."

"What? Wait? There's a second pair of Avatars?"

"Yes." The word came out in a hissing rumble. "The ones you know as Anna and Obsidian. They were created to battle the old Avatars if need be." The dragon stopped at the edge of the cliff and turned back to face Lord Draydrak and the assembly. Then he sat and gave everyone a look that said approach at one's peril.

"Oh, Hell. This is bad."

"Or it could be entertaining," the dragon countered, and Erika could sense his eagerness to see the coming fight. It appealed to the dragon's chaotic nature.

"Not entertaining," Erika muttered under her breath as she watched the old Avatars skeptically size up the new set.

CHAPTER THIRTEEN

Gregory

Staring across the expanse of sand, Gregory met Obsidian's gaze, and he saw the truth confirmed in the young male's gaze. Lord Death's words were true. He'd known Shadowlight had been spectacularly powerful for a premature gargoyle. And Anna had developed swiftly as well.

But back in the Mortal Realm, Gregory had been limited and hadn't seen the full potentials sleeping in the depths of their souls. But now? Now he could clearly see how powerful they were, how much more potential still waited within them, readying for a time it would be needed.

Still, he'd never imagined he was looking upon his and his lady's replacements. Even though he saw the truth in the youth's eyes and echoing in Lord Death's words, something didn't sit right with that knowledge in his mind.

If Anna and Shadowlight had been created to replace him and his Sorceress, why had they been reborn at all?

"Perhaps we are intended to mentor them?" Lillian suggested, though he sensed the doubt in her mind.

"I would do so gladly, but it still makes no sense. The Divine Ones could simply have given them the knowledge of everything they would need to know."

"Perhaps because the Lady of Battles interfered like she did with me?"

"Perhaps." But he still didn't fully accept that possibility. There was too much yet unknown.

"Gregory, my oldest mentor," Lord Death soothed, "you and your lady are more damaged by Gryton's creation than you know. While you and she have recovered a great deal, you still have a long journey until you are fully restored."

Gaze sharpening on Draydrak, Gregory huffed softly. That might be true... "But why did the Divine Ones not tell us this themselves?"

"Because the Lady of Battles found a way to steal what few memories you had from the time after Gryton's birth to now."

Gregory couldn't deny those words. His memory was spotty. So, too, was Lillian's.

"Have a care," she cautioned. *"I think this is a test."*

"A test?" But as he touched minds with her, he saw it as she did, and he agreed. It made sense if this was some sort of test to prove they were still capable of leading. *"I shall take care."*

He turned his attention back to Draydrak. "You say Anna and Obsidian are our replacements."

Draydrak gave him a mysterious smile. "I did not say that. I said both pairs must prove their worthiness to lead. The one I deem best suited will then become the commander of the Divine Ones' army."

"And is there a reason we can't just ask the Divine Ones which pair they'd prefer to lead?"

Draydrak's smile vanished. "You could. But the journey would take time and magical strength better used for preparing for the coming war. Perhaps a series of trials, such as what a novice, journeyman, and master must complete, only one more strenuous in light of an Avatar's greater power?"

"I knew I smelled a test," Lillian whispered in his mind. *"I still don't see the point. Even damaged from Gryton's birth, we would still easily win against Anna and Obsidian."*

Gregory huffed his agreement. But like Lillian, he detected something more hidden in Draydrak's words.

But just then Obsidian stepped forward and bowed to Lord Draydrak. "I shall battle Gregory if that is the will of the Divine Ones."

"He's going to get his ass kicked," Gran muttered to Thayn. "What foolery is this?"

Gregory probably wasn't meant to overhear, but he did anyway.

"I thank you." Draydrak bowed his head in acknowledgment of Obsidian's bravery. Then he turned to look at Gregory. "And you, Avatar? Will you face this young one in honorable combat?"

With a huff, Gregory took a step forward.

Behind him, Lillian made a sound of denial. *"What are you doing? You know as well as I do that winning a fight isn't going to win us the trial. There is always more to what Draydrak says than what's on the surface."*

"I know." He glanced over his shoulder and grinned at her.

He continued forward until he was in the center of the ring, facing a determined Obsidian. The youth's expression was a cross between determination and doubt that what he was about to do was wise.

"In your doubt, you show wisdom, Cub," Gregory sent along a private link, allowing his affection for the youth to cross over to the other male. Then he turned fully to face the Lord of the Underworld and said aloud, "I call your bluff. And will add that you have grown foolish since I last saw you if you think you can trick me, old friend. The Divine Ones may have created a second pair of Avatars, but it wasn't to battle us for supremacy."

Gregory smirked as Draydrak's ears slumped, betraying him. "If the Divine Ones did not think we were up to the role of leading their armies, they would have said as much in the Spirit Realm, and we would have bowed to their wisdom." He turned to look at the two youths. "However, I also trust their judgment. They created Anna and Obsidian for a purpose. I will not waste time fighting with my allies, but there is nothing to say the Avatars—either the new or the old—must lead alone. I welcome the new Avatars and ask them to rule beside my Sorceress and me."

"Hah! Told you they'd never fall for it," Thayn said with a good bit of glee. "You can pay up later, Dray."

Lord Draydrak merely smiled. "You won fairly. Come claim your reward whenever you wish."

Thayn huffed and then turned to grin at Gran. "I've won a great prize."

"And what prize would that be?"

"It shall be a surprise."

Gregory caught a hint of the elder's thoughts. Ah. Even his Sorceress hadn't yet realized what the old goat was up to.

Gran just shook her head at the elder's joy.

Suppressing a grin, Gregory turned his attention back to Draydrak. "So, if you had managed to convince me to fight Obsidian, what was going to be the lesson I was to have learned?"

"Besides the folly of allowing pride to lead you stumbling blindly into my trap?"

"Besides that, yes."

"Humility and that even the Avatars are not infallible and sometimes they need their friends to accomplish their goals. And perhaps to make you less hard-headed?"

"There might be something to that last part. I have been known for being hard-headed a time or two before," Gregory admitted. "And if the Divine Ones wished to teach me that I am not infallible, you need not reinforce that lesson. It's one I've already discovered. I've failed several times in this life already."

Draydrak spread his arms wide. "No one is perfect. Not you or me. Not your Sorceress. Not even the Divine Ones themselves, clearly. Otherwise, my twin would never have...."

"Gone off the rails?" Anna and Erika echoed in unison. They glanced at each other and then grinned.

"You will have to explain that phrase to me at some point," Lord Draydrak told the two women. "But there is something else we must talk of. Anna and Obsidian's true purpose. One I have not shared with them because I wanted you and your Sorceress to hear the rest of what I have to say first."

Lillian joined Gregory, and he instinctively curled a wing around her since she had returned to dryad form. Once he had her tucked against his side, he glanced up at Draydrak. "You have a tale you wish to tell?"

"I suppose I can begin it by saying that to truly serve the Light sometimes vows must be broken." Draydrak looked at the dragon when he said it. "When you and your Sorceress interrupted the Divine Ones' original plan, they had to come up with a new one. That is the real reason they created a second pair to act in the capacity of the Avatars. Anna and Obsidian were created to replace my twin and me."

Up until now, everyone in the assembly had been silent, listening attentively, but now the absolute stillness to the gathering spoke of deep shock. He glanced at Anna and Obsidian. By their near-identical expressions of surprise, he knew this was the first time they were hearing about this.

"I will help strip my twin's power from her and then give it to one of our young Avatars. Once my sister is sufficiently weakened, I will surrender my own power, and with yours and Lillian's help, we shall drag my twin back to the Spirit Realm for judgment and healing."

Draydrak paused. "If it is possible for her to be healed. Then, one day, we will return to take up the mantles of our power. If that isn't possible, then you and the Sorceress will perform your duties as the Avatars and bring two new demigods into being to take up my and my twin's magic. Until that time Anna and Obsidian will guard our respective powers."

"Holy. Fucking. Shit."

Gregory looked toward Anna. He couldn't blame her for the outburst. It was a surprising fate to have to swallow for one born not knowing anything of magic or the three realms. But he didn't doubt the Lord of the Underworld's words. Anna and Obsidian were both incredibly powerful. Now it made sense as to why. Even if they weren't destined to wield the power of death and war, merely provide the vessels in which to house the two powers, that was no small thing.

"Do we get a say in any of this?" Anna asked.

Draydrak bowed his head and smiled serenely. "Always. As with each new level of power and responsibility you have received, you have been granted a choice. You can accept this fate or deny it. The Divine Ones do not want slaves."

Anna snapped her teeth together, and Gregory was sure he heard them grind briefly before she spoke again. "Of course I'm going to say yes. My home is at risk."

Draydrak looked at Obsidian for long moments.

The gargoyle nodded. "I, too, agree."

"Very good. But even so, there are no guarantees of success."

"There never is," Anna said simply.

"No," Dray agreed.

Lillian stepped away from Gregory's side then and took command of the assembly. "If we're to win this war and finally defeat the Lady of Battles, we're going to need one ironclad plan. Let's start hashing this thing out."

And with his Sorceress giving no quarter, all parties began to discuss their strategy as the afternoon slid toward evening.

The sun was beginning its descent toward the ocean when Gryton stirred at last. Every set of eyes were drawn to the dragon as he shuddered a second time.

Erika reached up and touched the dragon's foreclaw as if seeking to comfort the great beast. But the dragon just gave his head a little shake and looked at Lillian.

"The Battle Goddess's captains have just awakened Gryton's sleeping Elites." The dragon's deep voice vibrated along Gregory's wing bones. "You should assume all the rest of her battalions are also waking. They will be battle worthy in less than four days."

Lillian glanced back at him; her eyes calm. She nodded, and he looked to the rest of the assembly. "Then we have less than that to march upon the Battle Goddess's kingdom."

The dragon nodded. "She'll strike the human world first, thinking we are still there. And there is another reason for her to attack the Mortal Realm first. They will seek to cause as much bloodshed as quickly as possible to feed the blood witch's spells. Killing humans will be far easier than killing gargoyles or other faebloods. If Taryin and the Battle Goddess manage to take the Earth, the witch will command a power as great as the Battle Goddess."

While usually, a blood witch couldn't hope to achieve that kind of power before the Light hunted her down, Gregory knew with a djinn and the Battle Goddess as her allies, this witch would have far more protection than any of her kin had ever possessed in the past.

Which must be the secondary reason the Divine Ones had sent such a powerful Null to pair up with the elemental dragon. Fire was destructive, but it was also a purifying force. The Null could weaken Taryin, and then the dragon would be able to burn away the witch's spells and then the witch herself.

Now if they could only gain the dragon's full cooperation.

CHAPTER FOURTEEN

Bervicta

All in all, things were going better than Bervicta would have thought. The Battle Goddess hadn't killed her or Vaspara or Sorac. Not yet, at least. Things looked to be improving. Not that their luck would last much beyond the opening skirmish in the coming war.

Bervicta didn't fool herself. She didn't expect all of them to survive. If given a choice, she'd surrender her own life to provide her two friends with a chance at a future with their draklings. She'd been surprised at how swiftly the little ones had worked their way into her heart, and she wanted them to have the best chance at survival. That meant Vaspara and Sorac needed to survive the war.

She just didn't know how to guarantee that outcome.

She was still mulling over unhappy thoughts when she

arrived at the drakling's nest deep below the fortress. Nodding sharply at the guards, she impatiently waited for them to release the ward spells and unlock the heavy iron-bound door. But soon the door was screeching open and she was striding through, her heart already feeling lighter at the thought of seeing the draklings again.

She was five steps inside the chamber when she stopped so suddenly, she nearly tripped. The draklings weren't alone.

Their other caregiver was present and turned to study her, his gaze like two pools of lava. The strange tattoos covering his muscular, bronze-toned body glowed with the same intensity as his eyes.

She still didn't know the djinn's name—didn't want to know it. It was said that to know a djinn's name was to have it hunt you down later, once it was free, and strip your soul of the knowledge. That just sounded painful and fatal.

Admitting she was terrified of the djinn wasn't hard in the quiet of her own mind.

Djinns were dangerous on a good day. This one had been summoned by a blood witch. Bervicta didn't know the particulars about what was being done to him when he wasn't here with the draklings, but she could see and feel the outcome. The witch's spells and magic were unbalancing the spirit being, tainting him with their darkness and madness. His mind was once shielded from Bervicta by his powerful magic, but now his shields would slip, and she'd get glimpses into his mind.

She wasn't sure if it was accidental or intentional. Both options were terrifying for different reasons. If accidental, then he was closer to insanity's cliff than she wanted to imagine. If intentional, then Bervicta had caught the creature's attention, and that was never a good situation.

Djinns were known to play with their victims before they killed them.

She usually tried to avoid the djinn when he was with the draklings, to give him time to find a bit of solace and balance in the chaos of his mind and to keep her own self out of the djinn's line of sight.

But today she'd been distracted and forgotten to check with the other guards on duty to see if the djinn was present. She thought about retreating back the way she'd come, but the draklings saw her and raced to her side. She'd been spending so much time with them, they'd come to accept her as a secondary mother.

When she glanced up to where the djinn had been standing, she realized he was gone. Oh, bloody, bloody balls.

She slowly straightened and turned her head. A beautifully sculpted, long-fingered hand cupped her face, and she was suddenly looking into his blazing eyes.

"Little harpy. You've been avoiding me." He looked her over, and for the first time she felt a shiver of fear course down her spine at a male's look of interest. "Did no one tell you trying to deny a djinn only piques our interest more?"

The terrifyingly beautiful male regarded her through half-lidded eyes. "And while I'm not normally interested in anything more than playing with my prey, there is something different about you today."

Leaning forward, the djinn sniffed along the skin of her jawline and down her neck.

"What are you doing? I damned well know a djinn isn't interested in sex with a harpy."

He smiled then, a look of glee in his expression. "You smell of my beloved companion—the Avatar. Or, at least, the female half of the soul. No other creature, demigod or flesh and blood would notice, she is so skilled at creating her spells. But I've known the Avatar soul my entire long existence. I know the touch and scent of its work. The female half has given you something for me. A gift."

Bervicta hastily stepped back. "I don't know what you're talking about."

"No. I don't suppose you do since the spell migrated to you from Vaspara. I scent her power upon the spell as well."

Bervicta's eyes widened at what he'd just revealed. If the Avatars had woven a spell upon Vaspara, that meant she hadn't escaped on her own. They'd let her go.

Was Vaspara helping them?

No. Not possible. They never would have injured an ally as severely as they did Vaspara that day. And yet if the djinn smelt one of the Sorceress's spells upon her, then she must have put it on Vaspara and then turned her loose with the intention she carry it here. To the djinn?

"Oh, yes, little harpy. This spell was intended for me from my oldest and most beloved companion."

Bervicta attempted to bolt for the door, but the djinn wrapped an arm around her waist and dragged her back. He was fiercely strong. Nothing should be that strong. She couldn't even wiggle in his grasp.

Leaning forward, he surprised her again by capturing her chin and forcing her to meet his lips. They were warm, hot even. A moment later he sucked on her, drawing out the spell and maybe a piece of her soul with it and then he was drinking down whatever spell the Avatars had smuggled into enemy territory.

"You are not the Sorceress, but when I close off my other senses and draw the Sorceress's spell from you, I can forget for a time that you aren't her."

But then he released her and Bervicta took a step toward the door.

He stalked forward, following her. "Perhaps if you'd spoken my name, it would have seemed more real." What she could only call a mischievous light entered his eyes. "Should I give you my name?"

"No." She continued to back up while he stalked her. She absolutely didn't want the monster's name so he could hunt her down later and exact his revenge.

He pinned her against the ironbound door. The iron reacted to his power, hissing and popping and igniting with sparks. Ignoring the iron, he leaned closer, his lips brushing against her ear. "I am Naharnin."

"No."

"Yes. I stand at the Avatar's side in the Spirit Realm. Its oldest friend, confidant, and beloved companion."

"Does the witch know what she has caught?"

"No." He paused and graced her with the most beautifully cruel smile she'd ever seen. He pressed a finger to her lips. "And you won't tell her or the Battle Goddess."

"I..." But suddenly she couldn't so much as think his name.

"And I wasn't caught, harpy. I came willingly."

She swallowed hard, only now realizing what the blood

witch's actions might bring down upon all their heads. The Avatars would level this fortress, destroy half a world to get this djinn back.

"Indeed, they will," the djinn whispered before he released his hold on his form and expanded into a cloud of shimmering power.

The draklings rushed over to him, and the djinn crooned happily to the little ones as they began to feed upon his magic.

Bervicta's hand slowly closed over the door's latch. As she worked upon the ward spell shielding the door, she pondered her options. She needed to find a way to kill the blood witch and get the djinn back into the hands of the Avatars.

They were the only ones with any hope of containing the monster the blood witch was driving mad.

CHAPTER FIFTEEN

Gregory

The Lord of the Underworld's home had likely seen more outsiders arrive on its shores in the last day than in the entirety of the last hundred thousand years. Human soldiers seemed to swarm everywhere as they helped Haven's gargoyles and dryads move supplies and weapons from the hidden city.

Earth's joint military once again performed with an efficiency that Gregory admired. They had set up a system of communication that crossed from the Mortal Realm into this world through an open portal spell and from here on to Haven.

The last step had been the trickiest, and Lillian needed to make a slight adjustment to the portal spell linking

Haven to the present time so that the humans' radio signals could travel back and forth without a delay.

Now a supply line moved from Haven to a temporary staging area outside of a human military base known as 22 Wing North Bay. From there, Second Legion would scatter into the surrounding forests under the guidance of human military leadership until they were ready to mobilize in a surprise attack on the Battle Goddess's temple.

It was a delicate time for the alliance with the gargoyles and dryads weak from stepping into the Mortal Realm for the first time, but Gregory had confidence in his human allies. After all, the humans would be just as dependent on the members of Second Legion when it was time to take the war to the Battle Goddess in the Magic Realm.

The knowledge that Anna and Obsidian had returned to the Mortal Realm with the first wave of the Second Legion and were overseeing things on that end put his mind at ease. The new Avatars were a capable pair.

New Avatars!

He was never going to get used to the idea that he and his Sorceress were no longer unique in the universe. Would Anna and Obsidian merge into a single soul at their deaths? He hoped they did. While there was pleasure to be experienced in flesh and blood forms and an unequaled delight in creating life and watching that child develop, there was nothing else like returning home and becoming complete once more.

But he also hoped that Anna and Obsidian survived the coming war and lived to enjoy a full, long life before experiencing what the Divine Ones had in store for them next.

"You, my beloved protector, are in an entirely too good

of a mood for one preparing for war," Lillian said as she stalked up to him and slid her arms around his waist.

He huffed softly. "I was not thinking of war. I was thinking of what we might all have to look forward to afterward should we all survive."

"You damn well better survive," she crooned as she leaned into him and pressed a kiss to his cheek.

He was just looking around for a place where they might find a few moments of privacy when magic flared up around his Sorceress. A look of delight crossed her face, and then she was reaching for his mind.

"My spell worked. It's Naharnin." Lillian closed her eyes, and Gregory did the same a moment later.

Instinctively his wings encircled her, and the spell continued to wrap around them. A moment later, he felt the tug on his soul.

"He wishes to speak in privacy, away from the other gargoyles," he said in sudden understanding.

"Wise of him. He doesn't want to see anything that he might later have to divulge to the witch."

"In that case..." Gregory called upon his gargoyle magic and turned both their bodies to stone before sending their spirits toward another location midway between the twins' temples.

When they first arrived in the place outside of time, there was nothing but emptiness. Then slowly, stars formed in the vast void of space. Nearer at hand a great blue star winked into existence, followed by a planet surrounded by many rings and several moons. The largest moon formed below where they stood.

Gregory recognized the place but allowed the djinn to

continue to construct it. Soon lush greenery and night-scented flowers appeared, growing along a wide stairway leading up to the temple of the Avatar.

All around them the night sky was aglow with nebulas and shooting stars and the glorious view of the ringed planet that this moon circled. Gregory and Lillian were standing on one of the viewing landings that they'd often used when they resided here. From this central point, they could look out into the universe in any direction.

Well, they could have if they'd been the Avatar soul. But being separated into two mortal bodies limited them, and they couldn't see much beyond the blue star, the planet, the moons, and the beautiful nebula against the black sea of space.

"I had forgotten the beauty of this place." Lillian's words came out in a breathy sort of awe.

"I think if we remembered too clearly what it is like when we are a single Avatar, we would miss this place too greatly."

Footsteps descended down the stairs behind them, and Gregory glanced over his shoulder just as a profoundly familiar voice wrapped around his mind.

"Perhaps that was a mistake on the Divine Ones' part. Maybe you should remember everything in detail." The djinn's tone held a hint of humor. "Perhaps then you wouldn't dally in the mortal or magic realms quite so long after completing a mission."

Lillian turned to watch the djinn, her warmth and love already reaching out for him. Gregory too stepped forward; his arms open wide. "Come here, you great showman. Give us a hug. We have missed our most ancient companion."

"I have missed you, too." Then the djinn rushed forward, power swirling around him. He reached Lillian first and scooped her up into his arms. She was wrapping her arms around him for a hug when the djinn captured her chin in his hand and stared into her eyes.

He caught the djinn's startling thoughts a moment before he was lowering his head to kiss the Sorceress. Several powerful sensations rushed through Gregory. Along with the surprising revelation that the djinn had been harboring some secret passion for the Sorceress, there was also warmth and love and the powerful bond of friendship.

At last, the djinn drew back, his gaze guarded once more. "I've always wanted to do that."

Gregory was surprised, but he wasn't angry or jealous. He actually found it touching.

Lillian and the djinn held an arm out for him, and he moved closer until he was wrapping them both in his embrace, his wings sheltering his other half and his oldest companion. It was perfect, this moment outside of time.

The djinn chuckled. "Had I known I'd have an easier time at seducing the Avatar soul while it was severed in two and housed in flesh and blood forms, I would have left the Spirit Realm and joined you much sooner. After all, it's certainly much harder to catch the eye of a sexless being in the Spirit Realm than two lovely flesh and blood bodies here in the Magic Realm."

The djinn purred the last words, and heat flushed Gregory's skin.

Lillian laughed in delight. "I think you just made my other half blush for the first time in his existence, Naharnin."

"Ah. My quest then is done." But a moment later all three of them turned sober.

They were all too aware they'd soon have to face each other from opposite sides of a battlefield.

"I do not want to fight you, my friends, but as the first-born of the djinn, I'm best able to resist the blood witch's influence longest. But even I can't hold out against her forever. You must bring the war to the Battle Goddess soon, or I will be lost to madness and no longer able to aid you."

Naharnin stepped back and glanced down at the magic swirling from his body. "As it is, it is already getting harder to influence the fleshlings around me. But I have been some-what successful in sowing discord among the ranks of our enemy's minions. None besides the Battle Goddess trusts the blood witch now. And while I have begun to exert influence upon her, I will not be able to continue much longer, not with the changes the blood magic attempts to make."

"You have done enough. Focus on your own battles and leave the demigoddess and her minions to us." Gregory rested a hand on the other's shoulder and gave it a squeeze.

Naharnin glanced up and met both their gazes. "I am sorry. I never want to hurt you. But be warned, if we meet in battle, the witch can force me to fight. And I beg you if I am too far gone to save when we next meet, allow the Null to kill me. I do not want my oldest and most beloved companion to have to do such a thing."

Gregory could feel Lillian's rage and pain. It reflected his own. "We will save you and the blood witch will regret ever enslaving a djinn."

A shudder ran through Naharnin's body, and his magic flared. For the first time, Gregory saw what the djinn attempted to hide from them. Reddish-brown coils of blood magic twisted and squirmed around the spirit being's form. He shuddered again.

"I am being summoned back to my vessel." Naharnin groaned in pain as his power fluctuated wildly.

Lillian gripped the djinn harder as if she could hold him by sheer force of will. But the djinn wasn't really here at all. There was nothing to hold onto.

But that knowledge didn't stop Gregory from reaching out and wrapping both Lillian and Naharnin in his wings once more as if he could hold the other male here against all laws of nature and magic.

Naharnin screamed and then convulsed, his form breaking apart like smoke and embers and ash. Then in the next heartbeat, he was gone and the place outside of time was gone with him.

Gregory once again stood on Draydrak's island, the humans, gargoyles, and dryads going about their business, unaware of what had just happened. In his arms, Lillian sobbed out her rage and anguish.

"We have to save him," she whispered in a broken voice. "Goddess, I could feel some of the things he's endured at the witch's hands. And he's still been attempting to aid us all this time.

"Shhh. We will find him and rescue him." Then his own rage slipped his control, and his voice lowered into a menacing growl. "No one will get away with harming Naharnin. I will find the blood witch and shred her soul and toss little tiny morsels into the void to feed the demons."

The destruction of a soul was the most serious of all punishments, and he'd only done such a thing three times before. Each time to a blood witch, their souls too far gone to save.

Because sometimes evil just needed to be cast into the void.

CHAPTER SIXTEEN

Lillian

After the brief meeting with Naharnin, she'd needed something to distract her from her impotent rage and anguish, which was why Lillian was now walking down one of the beautiful sand beaches surrounding the island. She was on her way to meet up with Gryton and Private Emerson while Gregory was busy seeing that each of the gargoyle council members knew to which of the human command units they needed to report.

Focusing on Gryton—or the dragon as it were—helped her regain her balance. It had been strange seeing Naharnin while she and Gregory were flesh and blood, and it became equally apparent that while they'd never thought of him as a sexual being, he most certainly was.

In the past, he'd always just been part of their existence

as the Avatar. But like all djinn, he did have a gender even though he had never taken on a flesh and blood form to beget offspring with another djinn. When she was the Avatar, she and her other half had always assumed it was because Naharnin preferred to stay in an incorporeal form in the Spirit Realm, that he didn't like surrendering power to take on a mortal body.

Now she thought it was something else entirely.

"Gregory, how could we be so blind?"

His thoughts touched hers, reading what she'd been dwelling on. *"It wasn't blindness. In the Spirit Realm, the Avatar saw things differently. We knew of his love and loved him in return. Do you deny that the Avatar loved Naharnin?"*

"No." She sighed in frustration, though not at Gregory. It was at her own unsettled emotions. *"But I'm only now realizing that he loved the Avatar in a much different way."*

"Yes. Like you, I was unaware of the depth of Naharnin's... desires. He either hid them very well, or—and I think this more likely—the djinn has only recently realized his feelings." Gregory paused, and she could feel him sorting through their many lifetimes of memories and experiences. *"I think the events of our last life—when it became apparent to him that we might not always be around—frightened him into admitting his own feelings for the first time."*

"He tried to emulate us until he denied his own drives and needs, didn't he?"

"I believe so." There was another long pause, and then her Gargoyle Protector surprised her. *"After this life is over and we are once again one being in the Spirit Realm, we will seek out Naharnin and face this new—or perhaps very old—develop-*

ment and find a solution that fulfills everyone's needs. Perhaps the Divine Ones will create a mate for Naharnin if we ask them?"

Hmmm. A mate? Lillian dwelled on her beloved's words even after he was gone. "Oh, you great clueless male, I think the Divine Ones have already selected a mate for poor Naharnin but said mate was too self-centered to look outside itself and too self-absorbed with its duties and responsibilities to the Divine Ones to notice that Naharnin might wish for something besides platonic companionship.

But her gargoyle was correct. Some things would have to wait until after this life was over, but that didn't mean she wasn't going to have a long chat with the djinn as soon as she rescued him and healed him from whatever the monstrous witch was working upon him.

Lillian eventually found her elemental dragon son on a spit of land on the north end of the island.

"What seems to be the problem?" she asked with a chuckle.

Erika looked over her shoulder, looking tired and a bit defeated. "Gryton doesn't like the dragon and the dragon doesn't like Gryton. I can't convince the dragon to shift back even though I explained we want to keep his presence a secret until we're ready to fight the Lady of Battles."

"You could have come to me for help."

Erika lowered her voice. "He won't let me leave his side any farther than to go pee behind some rocks if I'm lucky."

Lillian looked up at the dragon. "And why haven't you

come to visit your mother instead of giving your poor Null a hard time?"

The dragon gave her a somewhat sheepish look but didn't respond.

Private Emerson cleared her throat loudly and then elbowed the dragon in the shin. "The one thing both Gryton and the dragon agree on is that they distrust Lord Draydrak. I think that's the real reason the dragon will not shift back."

"Well, at least they agree on something." Lillian arched her brows at the dragon. "While you are a very handsome fellow and magnificent to look upon, and I'm not just saying that because I'm your mother, Erika isn't wrong. You need to—"

She'd been about to say surrender but caught herself, remembering how competitive the dragon was, and as much as the dragon side of her son's nature didn't like the more controlled and logical Gryton, the dragon was much like Gryton because they were two sides of the same being. Gryton never surrendered. And neither would the dragon.

After scrounging around for the correct wording, she smiled up at the dragon. "For our side to have a chance to win this coming war without massive bloodshed, we need a few surprises up our sleeves. And you, mighty dragon, are the greatest surprise. But we'll only maintain that element if we can keep you a secret. As soon as you leave these waters, the Battle Goddess's spies will be sure to discover you."

The dragon snorted a sound of disdain.

"Think of the fear you'll inspire in our enemies the first time they see you flying into battle with a Null of the First

Wave riding on your back. More than a few of the Battle Goddess's soldiers will surely run in terror. The chaos you create will be impressive."

The dragon preened a little and then nuzzled Erika right off her feet.

While the human soldier was picking herself up off the damp sand and cursing most creatively about 'damned fools' and 'little boys needing a good whoopin' from their mama' Lillian continued.

"But that delightful advantage will be ruined if they learn of your existence. The only way to cause the chaos of that vision is if you give Gryton control again for a time. Let him deal with the tedium of military staging and strategy and moving soldiers around like pieces on a chessboard. Then when it's time to kill things, you take command, for you are less vulnerable than the two-legged version of my son. And I most certainly want you to survive the coming war."

The dragon made a happy sort of rumble and then in the next moment, fire was bursting to life all along his scales. The human soldiers assigned to watch the dragon and Erika came to attention, their hands tightening on their weapons. But Erika gestured them back, and they eased a few steps away, though Lillian noted they wisely didn't let their guard down.

The dragon was still far too volatile to trust.

But this time, the dragon had heeded her words, and as the fire shrunk down upon itself, the air soon grew cooler, and a naked Gryton was kneeling in the sand. Lillian looked out to the ocean to give her son a moment to compose himself.

"I swear the dragon leaves me naked intentionally." The words were growled out as Gryton stood and walked into her peripheral vision.

Erika muttered under her breath about getting blinded by the moon and Lillian had to fight back a laugh at her son's expense. Gryton's fire magic flared. She gave him another moment before she faced him. He was once again covered in his scaled armor.

"Mother, you may have successfully bargained with the dragon this time, but you won't always have something that appeals to the beast."

"That is true."

"It is dangerous. You can't trust it. It is a deceptive creature," he cautioned.

"Actually, you're wrong. I have met few beings as honest as your dragon. He's very clear about his dislikes."

Gryton snorted. "Very well. You have me there. The beast will gladly tell you it means to destroy entire realms if it can manage the feat. You can't trust it. If you know of some way to bind it so it can never break free again once we no longer need it, then you must tell me how."

She pinned her son with a look and then turned and started to walk down the beach. Lillian waited until Gryton figured out he was supposed to follow before she continued. "Leashing the dragon is not an option. Put that out of your head now. And the dragon is not a separate beast. He is you. A part that you've long denied out of fear."

Gryton snorted. "I've denied it so that it doesn't destroy entire kingdoms."

"I know. But I am here now and together with the

Null's help, you will learn to merge the dragon with this personality."

"This personality is me."

"I assure you; the dragon believes the same of himself. But you are both aspects of my son. And you are strong. You will master yourself and be whole. Then you'll be truly formidable."

"If the dragon doesn't win," Gryton muttered darkly.

CHAPTER SEVENTEEN

Lillian

Gregory hadn't yet returned from Haven, and Lillian found herself inside one of the humans' mess tents that had been set up on a terrace on the north slope of the extinct volcano. The tent's one wall was rolled up. Above them Draydrak's temple sat pristine and majestic. The surrounding gardens had been trampled, but a few crushed flowers would be the least of Draydrak's worries if they didn't win this war.

Lillian sat on a wooden plank that was propped up on two large buckets. Beside her on the impromptu bench, Gryton sat and nursed a cup of coffee. He didn't like it, but it was hot, and he hated cold drinks.

It was one of the little things she'd learned about her son. And she was surprised how happy unearthing little tidbits like that made her. Though she knew not to show it. Gryton kept a shield around his emotions and didn't want anyone getting in. Not even her.

Private Emerson sat on Gryton's other side. Gran, Thayn, Major Resnick, and Sergeant Maracle sat on the opposite bench. Her son glowered at the three opposite him every other sip of his coffee.

Lillian took a drink from her cup to hide a smile and winced. "Goddess, this really is terrible stuff."

"Coffee's fine. You're just used to Gran's magic food," Erika said from Gryton's other side.

Everyone at the table turned to look at the Null.

Gryton's head jerked up. "Magic food?"

"Magic what?" Resnick uttered just before he dropped his head into his hands. "I don't want to be hearing about this now."

Erika looked up with surprise. "You mean y'all didn't know Gran spikes her food with magic?"

Gran looked equal parts unhappy and guilty. Lillian had only recently learned that her grandmother had been enchanting her food after she'd returned to Earth following Gryton's rescue. Gregory, food-oriented creature that he was, had known Gran's secret but hadn't seen the need to put her on the spot and risk his favorite cook growing angry at him.

Which now left Lillian with the task of delicately explaining the situation to Major Resnick.

Thayn grunted, coming to Gran's defense. "It's just a little magical flavoring. Not much different than sprinkling herbs and spices on your food. It certainly isn't any more harmful than what you humans normally eat."

The major studied Thayn for a moment and then looked back at Lillian. "He's telling the truth?"

"Yes and no. Yes, her magic infuses all her work. But as Thayn said, it mostly just enhances flavor."

"Mostly?" Resnick was looking unhappier by the second.

"Sometimes she puts a little something extra in the food. It merely helps put people in a good mood and fosters cooperation."

"She roofies the food?" Major Resnick stood up and held out a hand. "Stop talking. I don't want to hear any more right now. We have enough problems to handle. I'll wait to write this up after the war is over." He paused and glowered at Gran. "Your word you won't feed anything else to my men or any other humans?"

Gran nodded. "You have my word."

"Good." Resnick rose from the bench and started away. He glanced back and grumbled something unintelligible at Sergeant Maracle. The sergeant jumped up and was almost out of the tent when he doubled back and grabbed two handfuls of cookies from the table.

"Evidence?" Lillian asked. "Gran really wasn't doing anything nefarious."

"Hell no." Maracle snorted. "These are for me."

Then he was hurrying to catch up with Resnick. Erika was rising to follow and then paused when she noticed Gryton was still sitting on the bench. "You have to come with me, Hot Stuff. That's the deal to keep you out of a cage."

Gryton grunted but grabbed a selection of the food from Gran's potluck.

"I'll see you later," Lillian called after Gryton and Erika.

He paused and looked over his shoulder at her. "Make sure you do. I don't fancy having to be surrounded by humans for the rest of the day."

Gran rose a short time later. "I should take something to Gregory to make sure he eats. A hungry gargoyle is a grumpy gargoyle."

Thayn grinned and started to rise as well. "Let me help with carrying things for you."

Lillian's eyes narrowed. Thayn had been acting odd since he'd first arrived in the Mortal Realm. She'd thought things would return to normal once he was home, but that wasn't the case. "Thayn, can you stay a moment. I'd like to discuss something with you."

Thayn glanced at her and must have seen something on her face, for his expression turned serious. "Of course, Avatar."

Gran gave them both long looks, but merely gathered up some items for Gregory and then headed off.

"What's going on between you and Gran?"

Thayn's ears tilted to the side, showing his embarrassment. "I was that obvious?"

"Yes. Though I don't understand this sudden infatuation with Gran. Not that she isn't a wonderful person, but you barely know her."

"That's just the thing. I do know her. I've known her for a very long time. She is Marnideen reborn."

Lillian froze. Marnideen? Thayn's long lost dryad mate?

As the Sorceress, she had known Thayn's dryad mate across more than one lifetime. But to Thayn's great sorrow Marnideen had been killed in a raid by their enemies. She'd died and made the journey to the Spirit Realm well over eight thousand years ago.

"You're sure?"

"Yes. And it makes perfect sense. The Divine Ones needed a soul they knew they could trust to guide, protect, and raise you once you came to the Mortal Realm."

"Oh, Thayn. I don't know if I should be glad for you or grieve on your behalf. Gran is human with only a little faeblood in her background. She'll live another hundred years at most." Lillian's throat tightened for him. The grief he would feel at her loss and separation would be terrible. And yet Thayn enjoyed life too much to seek to end his own.

"Be glad for I am reunited with my love at last."

"But it will only be for a short time."

"I would rather have these few short years than none at all."

"Of course. And I am happy for you. I just wish there was a way to extend Gran's life by means within the Light."

Thayn cleared his throat. "I may have solved that."

Lillian narrowed her eyes. "Does this have anything to do with that bet with Draydrak?"

"Yes." He fell silent and looked at her expectantly. "Aren't you going to ask me what I won?"

Lillian folded her hands and rested her chin upon them. "My dearest Thayn. I know you too well. I assume you extorted some promise to make Gran immortal."

He huffed. "You make it sound far easier than it was."

Lillian laughed and then stood and came up behind the oldest of the gargoyles. She hugged him, ending by placing a kiss on the top of his head. "I am happy for you and her.

Just don't turn her into some kind of deathless zombie. She'd never let you hear the end of it if you do."

Thayn choked on his drink. Once he was finished sputtering, he looked over his shoulder and just shook his head. "Rest assured, it is nothing of darkness."

Lillian started from the tent and then stopped. "And make sure Gran knows who and what you are and what you and Draydrak have concocted. Gran hates being kept out of the loop."

"I know. I just haven't come up with the right words to tell her."

"It's obvious she cares for you. Just go on and spit the words out. They'll likely come as a relief. She is astute. She'll have sensed something familiar about you. Your words will explain what she hasn't been able to discover for herself." Lillian paused. "And there are no guarantees in war. You should tell her soon."

"I will." Thayn no longer sounded hesitant. "I shall go now and seek her out and tell her the truth."

Despite not knowing the future, Lillian couldn't believe the Divine Ones had only brought them together again after all this time to break them apart so soon. She was grinning when she left the tent. Gran deserved happiness, and she could do much worse than Thayn. And her oldest gargoyle friend deserved happiness again at last as well.

CHAPTER EIGHTEEN

Erika

The gathering and transporting of the Second Legion to Earth from Haven took a little over two days. They couldn't send the entire two hundred thousand strong membership in one shot. The quantity of magic it would take to power such a massive portal spell would be noticed by their enemies.

So, the sixty thousand gargoyles and the one hundred and forty thousand dryads had to make the trip in much smaller numbers.

And while Erika thought that was an impressive number of gargoyles, she'd also learned from Gryton that the Battle Goddess's army numbered around eight hundred thousand.

As Erika stood with Major Resnick's team in the

company of Thayn, Gran, and Jason, she watched the last group of gargoyles and dryads vanish through the portal spell with misgivings.

"As impressive as all those gargoyles are, unless I'm much worse at math than I think I am, we're still badly outnumbered." Erika hadn't directed the question at anyone in particular but Adept Thayn leaned forward around Gryton to peer at her.

"It will be a fair fight. One gargoyle is worth any three of the Battle Goddess's soldiers."

"It depends on the soldier," Gryton commented dryly. "But with the Battle Goddess, Blood Witch Taryin, and the oldest of the djinn versus the Avatars, Lord Death, and the Null and me, both sides are fairly evenly matched. It could easily be a blood bath that could end in yet another stalemate if not for the alliance my parents brokered with your kind."

Major Resnick grunted. "Yeah. Remind me again why we're lining up to get ass reamed?"

The major's words were more a comment than a question, but after a pause, where Erika could almost feel Gryton working out the meaning of Resnick's slang, he answered, his expression serious.

"Because the Battle Goddess already attempted to destroy your planet with my death. If my parents had not stopped her, your world would be cosmic dust. And if your kind pulls out of this alliance and the battle ends in a stalemate again, the Battle Goddess will one day seek to rebuild her army, and your world is not without its uses. She would loose her warriors upon your populous to feed and breed."

Resnick mouthed the last three words and then shook his head. "I didn't need that visual."

"If Fate is merciful, you need not ever see such atrocities firsthand."

But the last group was making their way to the portal, and now it was Erika and her companion's turn. They were headed back to Earth, where they would wait for word from the scouting teams made up of dryad scouts and human special forces.

When Erika crossed through the portal spell and came out the other side, it was to find night had fallen here as well. Though the military base was still teaming with activity. Major Resnick and his men remained to act as Gryton's guards until Anna and Obsidian arrived with their own team of gargoyles.

"Major," Anna said and then saluted him, "We're to guard Gryton while you report to command."

"I'm headed there now." Resnick nodded, sounding tired but also still determined. I assume you've already secured lodgings for Gryton?"

The way Resnick said lodgings, Erika pictured another clear-walled cage.

"Yes, sir. Everything is ready."

With that, Erika's group split up. She and Gryton followed Anna and Obsidian and the new guards while Major Resnick and his men headed off to command. Gran, Jason, and Thayn headed off to meet the clan and coven members already gathering in the forest outside of the military base with the newly arrived Second Legion.

To Erika's great surprise, and Gryton's too, the fire elemental wasn't to be housed in a cage on base. They were led out into the forest and soon came to a site where other gargoyles and dryads were already setting up their temporary homes.

"You both will stay here," Anna said as she pointed to one tent before turning a glower upon Gryton. "Everyone agreed that the gargoyles are better guards for you, but don't think to cause trouble because you are under surveillance. If you so much as step one toe out of line, you'll find yourself back in a cage before you have time to wonder what happened. Do I make myself clear?"

Gryton nodded, but Erika sensed he wanted to say something else, something to Anna. She was just reaching for his thoughts to tell him to mind his own business, but he beat her to it.

"Anna, might I have a word alone? There is something I wish to speak with you ab—"

"No," Anna's expression had closed down. No emotion showed, but there was a hard edge to her voice. "There is nothing you need to say to me that Obsidian can't hear. And to clarify things I'll add that there is never going to be an us, Gryton. I feel nothing toward you. If you weren't the Avatars' son, I would have seen you into some dark prison hole on some abandoned world for what your actions caused. Shadowlight was captured because of you."

Obsidian reached out and placed a hand on her shoulder. "Anna, that's enough."

Anna shook off his hand. "Gryton, if you don't stop sniffing after me, I swear I'll be your doom. There is no way I'll ever pick you. I'll always pick Obsidian. Every damn time. He's my Rasoren. My partner. My friend.

Keeper of my heart. I know I can always trust him. You, on the other hand, are the least trustworthy creature I know."

Erika knew the other woman had reason to dislike Gryton, but she still felt sorry for him. Though, the last thing he'd want would be her pity, so she just stood without comment.

"You have made yourself clear, Anna of the gargoyles." Gryton bowed deeply and then turned and walked into the tent.

As soon as he was inside, Anna turned and stalked off. Erika was left staring at a startled Obsidian. He had that look a guy got when he learned the woman he loved returned his feelings.

"You didn't know how she felt?"

"I knew. But it's complicated, and I hadn't thought to ever hear her admit to choosing me. Anna was in love once before, and it didn't end well, and then there was a secondary trauma."

"Well, in that case, you should probably go after her and offer comfort or something. I'm no expert, but I think Anna said things she hadn't really faced yet herself."

"You are likely more of an expert than many. Thank you for your words of wisdom, Ancient One." With that, the big male gave himself a shake and followed Anna.

Erika still wasn't sure about the 'ancient one' thing, but she wished them well. They seemed like a good match, their relationship already full of friendship and love.

With a sigh, she turned to face the tent where Gryton had vanished. And by Anna's earlier words, apparently, this was supposed to be Erika's tent as well. Great. Guess no one was taking a chance that the dragon might try to overcome Gryton and put in an appearance while they were on Earth.

But more importantly, she imagined Gryton could probably use a friend even if he didn't want one.

"You decent? I'm coming in," she shouted.

Gryton was tempted to answer with a 'no' and shed his scale armor if it would keep her away, but she was already shouldering her way inside. She took a moment to allow her sight to adjust to the darkness, and then she stomped over to where he was sitting on a cot. After a moment staring down at him, she turned and settled beside him until they were shoulder to shoulder.

Surprisingly, she didn't say anything. Just sat there next to him, not even feeding.

It was actually rather nice, he admitted in secret. And the dragon liked having her close. The beast hadn't been pleased to return to the Mortal Realm—something to do with how it limited the dragon's ability to touch the Null.

Gryton never thought he'd have something to be thankful to the Mortal Realm for. But if the Mortal Realm could limit the dragon, he'd look for ways to remain here after the war.

As he sat there next to her, a strange thing happened. The urge to unburden himself was strong enough he inhaled a deep breath and then began to speak.

"I wasn't trying to get her into my bed." A bitter laugh escaped him. "I was going to apologize for my behavior, of all things."

Erika merely leaned back and turned her head to study his profile.

He tucked his chin, but the words just kept pouring out. "I could not have her even if I wanted to. The dragon hates her."

Beside him, Erika stiffened and then turned more fully to him.

"Why does the dragon hate her, and is she in danger?"

Gryton snorted again. "Everyone is in danger from the dragon. That's what I've been trying to tell you and my mother."

"I mean why does he suddenly hate Anna in particular? Why is he singling her out? Because she rejected you? If so, I'll have to warn the others."

Oh, the innocent and clueless Null. How could one of the First Wave be so naïve? "The dragon doesn't hate her because she spurned my advances. He hates her because I showed interest in her. But the beast wants me to court another."

"Who?" she asked with growing suspicion in her tone.

"You."

The Null jerked like he'd tossed cold water on her.

"Oh, hell! No."

"The dragon cares nothing for denials, I've discovered." Gryton looked Erika over, trying to see what the dragon saw in her. But he knew it wasn't something visible to the naked eye. "He wants me to court you. I shall fight any power that tries to control or enslave me, but I doubt I'll be able to win. The dragon has proven himself stronger."

"Well, I'm a Null. I'm not helpless. If the dragon gets

too friendly, I'll suck him dry and let him stew on the error of his ways."

"Don't bother lying to me, Null. I know you've lost control over a part of your power, and you can't feed on the dragon."

"Fine. You got me there. But why does the dragon even care about me in that way? What possible benefit can there be for him?"

Gryton snorted. "I am a creature born of the Avatars. The dragon is a demigod in his own right. And yet there are no others like him."

"Amen to that."

"I believe he wishes to change that."

"Change it how?"

"He wishes to breed with you."

The Null choked and sputtered until he thought she'd swallowed her tongue.

"Why the actual fuck would you think that?"

"Because I was in his head. I saw his desires for the future. Amid the wish for chaos and destruction, there was also a dragon's drive to find his mate and produce offspring."

"Hell, nobody wants that. How do we make sure that the dragon doesn't take our choices and force the issue?"

"I do not know, but the first step is me winning against the dragon."

"Maybe if I explain to the dragon what asexual means, that I don't feel any more romantic toward you than I do my rifle, he'll leave us alone?"

Gryton snorted with humor. "That won't matter to the dragon."

"Damn it. And here I was starting to like the dragon more than you. Guess I'm going to have to rethink that."

"And that is the first bit of wisdom you've shown since I met you."

She rolled her eyes at him and then turned serious. "All jokes aside, if you need a friend to help you battle the beast, I'm your girl."

"Has no one told you I don't have friends." Gryton surprised himself again by adding, "But I will keep your offer in mind."

"Anyway, while you debate with yourself about whether to accept my friendship or not, I'm going to bed. Morning is only a few hours off, and you'll be needed to help with magic-proofing all the military vehicles and ordnance."

"Goodnight, Null."

In truth, he was glad of her friendship. He thought he might need it in the years to come when everything he'd known turned to ash, and he had to rebuild and reshape himself into something new. To do that he needed to reach some kind of a compromise with the dragon before it took all his choices away.

But first, they had a war to win. If they lost, Gryton might not have long to worry about the dragon. The Battle Goddess would see them both dead, and the Null along with him. The thought of the Null's death bothered him a great deal, and he found himself glancing across the tent to the other cot where Erika was already asleep.

"You're entirely too trusting, my Null."

CHAPTER NINETEEN

Lillian

Slipping silently through the forested slopes of the valley, Lillian made her way to the edge of the trees. Gregory was a silent shadow beside her. Behind them, the First Legion spread out along the tree line, as silent as she and Gregory had been. Secrecy and stealth were of the utmost importance until they were ready to strike.

The advanced scouts led by Master Rook had been swift to capture and contain the enemy scouts and patrols. Then they'd brought each one to Lillian, and she'd placed powerful spells upon them, preventing them from betraying the presence of the First Legion while still allowing the enemy scouts to report the all clear along a mental link back to their commander in the fortress city.

The first part of the plan was going well. They were nearly in place and still hadn't been discovered. With Light's army split in two, it was a delicate time. They needed to avoid discovery until the Battle Goddess had committed to opening the massive portal spells she planned to use to transport her army to Earth.

Such an expenditure of power would weaken both the Battle Goddess and Blood Witch Taryin temporarily. Meanwhile, Anna and Obsidian would be on Earth waiting with Second Legion for Lillian to commandeer the portal spells and direct them to where she wanted them, not where the demigoddess and witch planned. And when the portals opened, they would be very surprised to find the Second Legion, the human military, and the Clan and the Coven waiting for them.

Lillian grinned.

"What is that look for, my beloved?"

She turned to her gargoyle protector. "Just imagining the Battle Goddess's expression when she meets Second Legion.

After Anna and Obsidian led Second Legion through, the clan and coven would follow. Those two factions would then drive back the Battle Goddess's army enough to give the human military a window to mobilize and cross the portal, leaving Gryton and Private Emerson last. They didn't want the Null's power to disrupt the portal spell until all three groups were safely across.

If the portal survived Erika's crossing—Lillian intended to make sure it did—then the unmanned drones and other air support would make use of the gateway.

Then they would attack the Battle Goddess on two

fronts and crush her army between them. Of course battles didn't always go as planned.

Lillian gave a mental snort. *And that may well be the easy part.*

Only after the armies were engaged and Lillian and Gregory had managed to clear a path to the Battle Goddess's temple would the Lord of the Underworld leave his island home for the first time in an age. As soon as Lord Draydrak summoned a portal spell, that would be the signal for Gryton and Erika to join the fight. Unless they were needed sooner.

The surprise attack would sweep through the enemy's line of defense, and then together both sets of the Avatars as well as Gryton and Erika would face Naharnin, the Battle Goddess, and Blood Witch Taryin. During that phase of the battle, Light's army would fall back to a safe distance, for once Death joined the fight, it wouldn't be safe for anyone other than a demigod or a Null to be too near the fighting.

There was a slight rustle behind her, and Master Rook appeared. She knew the rustle was him being polite. He was too well trained to stir so much as a leaf as he moved toward them.

"Sorceress. Protector." He gave each of them a bow. "There is another large group coming up behind us. They were using concealing magic. Otherwise, we would have sensed them much sooner."

"Who are they?" Gregory asked.

"Other Faebloods."

Gregory huffed. "I suppose we shouldn't be surprised.

The sidhe are nearly as good at sniffing out an intruder on their lands as a gargoyle is at sniffing out an enemy."

"Told you we should have given them some reason for why we were crossing their lands." Lillian smirked at her other half.

"No matter what we told them, if we had revealed ourselves in advance of the crossing, they would have guessed the real reason—the only reason—the Legion would be seen marching in the direction of the Battle Goddess's kingdom. And we couldn't risk spies learning of it in advance. Now, even if there were spies in the sidhe lands, they'll have no way to send a message via magical means through the wards I put in place, and nothing is faster than a gargoyle on foot, not even their fae horses."

"Well, they caught up and are here now. I know they're spoiling for a fight." Rook commented, a stern expression on his face. "Our spies report that the Battle Goddess's patrols have been making raids on their territory to snatch innocent fae to feed the witch's spells. We couldn't do anything about it and risk inciting a war until all was in place." He made a husky sound of displeasure. "I hated sitting and doing nothing."

"Go. Tell them they are most welcome to join our cause, but warn them to stay along the outskirts, clearing up the numerous enemy we miss. I don't want them caught unaware when Lord Draydrak arrives." Gregory paused and grunted, his tone turning darker. "And ultimately, this battle will be between demigods and creatures of equal strength."

"I understand." Rook bowed and then vanished back the way he'd come.

"The sidhe deserve to be here," Lillian said after Rook had gone to carry out his orders. "They, too, have lost much in skirmishes with the Battle Goddess. This will fulfill their need to at last avenge loved ones."

"Let us all hope that we don't lose too many of our loved ones in this war."

Gregory belly crawled a few feet and then halted until Lillian and Greenborrow caught up with him. They and the rest of the legion gargoyles had been doing the same for most of the morning until they were now midway down the treeless slopes overlooking the valley floor. Below them, the Battle Goddess's army spread out like a dark and shifting sea.

That dark sea had been growing larger since they'd first set eyes upon it, more soldiers arriving through smaller portals, returning from other already conquered lands. If Gregory had his way, those warriors would never be returning to those enslaved kingdoms.

If this battle went well, an entire empire of enslaved worlds would once again know freedom.

When he deemed the legion's shadow magic could flow another few feet down the slopes without triggering a disturbance in the natural flows of magic here, he gave the silent order to continue.

They were almost close enough that his Sorceress would be able to reach out and steal control of the portal spells now being built. While she did that, he planned to start a war. And while he was off fighting enemy soldiers to create a distraction, Greenborrow along with some of the council would stay close to Lillian and act as bodyguards just in case the enemy broke through the line.

He didn't expect such an outcome—he planned to kill anyone who got too close to his Sorceress himself. But a contingency plan was never amiss.

The wait wouldn't be long now. Already a line of three separate walls of power shimmered in front of the Battle Goddess's army. To judge by the level of power swirling in the core of each spell, they would be finished and capable of carrying an army to the Mortal Realm shortly.

"Are you ready?" he asked along their private link.

"I'm always ready to make the Battle Goddess have a bad day."

Gregory had to fight back a laugh. It didn't help when Rook gave him a dark glower as if he'd seen Gregory's chest shaking in silent mirth. The look didn't help, but he mastered himself and started down a few more feet, being sure his shadow magic hid the unnatural movement of the grasses. It helped that there was a breeze. He could easily match the grasses' movements to the shifting air currents.

To both sides, the other gargoyles were doing the same while carrying a double load of dryad riders. Once the battle was engaged, the dryads would take to the ground, freeing the gargoyles to fight on foot alongside them or in the air as needed.

"There," Lillian said directly into his mind. *"On the steps. There's the blood witch..."*

Lillian's words trailed off as her eyes settled on the figure behind the witch. It was the djinn.

Naharnin, we will rescue you or free you to return to the spirit realm, Gregory vowed.

"I don't see or sense the vessel the witch would have used to trap the djinn," Lillian said, sounding more annoyed than worried about that fact. "No matter. It will be near. I'll find it."

"I can't sense Naharnin even though he's in sight." Gregory wasn't sure how that was possible, but he didn't like the new development. In the past, he'd always been able to sense a trapped djinn. Was this one of the ways he'd been weakened after Gryton's birth?

What other ways was he now less? On the battlefield was never a good place to learn such things.

Alas, the witch soon reached the bottom of the stairway and began walking through the town at its base. Gregory's eyes narrowed. He didn't remember anything in the reports about a village here. But the witch was soon through the town and already moving swiftly toward the portal spells where they waited in standby mode. She hadn't even reached the three walls of shimmering power before she began to feed more magic into them. But that wasn't what caught his attention. A secondary power stirred along his senses. This wasn't the witch or the djinn.

Gregory glanced back up the slope where the red stairs rose up into the fortress city. Rich blue magic with ribbons of darkness swirling through it flowed down the stairs, cascading over the steps like water over rocks.

It would have been pretty if he hadn't known the source.

The Lady of Battles was adding her own power to the portal spell. With the added energy, the portals were once again growing in size. The great workings of magic thrummed like the deepest tone of a war harp.

"Now," Lillian shouted as she rose up and dropped her cloaking shadow magic cover.

All along the slope, gargoyles and dryads rose up with her, summoning battle magic. Gregory joined them, a great spear of power forming in his hands. Screaming a challenge, he took to the air and winged his way down the slope. The fastest fliers in the legion followed on his tail.

Picking out his first target, he loosed his spear and took down a great troll of a creature. There were likely many far deadlier monsters, but the beast had already been running up the slope toward Gregory's Sorceress.

No one would touch her while he lived.

As if sensing Lillian's presence even surrounded by the legion racing forward to do battle, several of the nearest enemy battalions launched their own magical attack in the vicinity of his Sorceress. The first wave of weaponized magic hit the shield he'd erected around her and then he was roaring a second challenge, unleashing waves of deadly shadow magic as he flew.

The dark wave raced across the sky ahead of him for several heartbeats before it twisted in the air and arrowed down, impaling the leading edge of the enemy army. In a part of his mind not directed at the battle, he felt his lady summon an even greater wave of magic.

"Destroy all those with evil intent, my Lady."

"Oh, you want to destroy Earth, do you?" Lillian asked the blood witch even though she knew the other woman wouldn't be able to hear her over the battle magic being hurled back and forth. "Well, I have a little surprise for you."

Reaching out with a vast wave of raw spirit magic, she shaped the power to her will. Moments later, her magic collided with the first of the portal spells and merged with it. Shortly, her power reached the next two and sank into their complex weavings.

"Yes. That's it," she crooned as she instructed her vastly stronger power to take command of the portal spells. "You're mine now."

Grinning a toothy gargoyle grin, she looked to the startled blood witch and sent her words flying to the other woman's ear. "You are a green amateur compared to me, Witch. Let me show you what true power feels like and what it can do to one's enemies."

She closed her eyes and spread her wings, power rising up from her body and flowing down from above as she drew energy from the fissure she'd opened. The force continued to build until her wings shook with the strain of containing it. Then with a shout of joy, she loosed another wave of pure spirit magic at the witch.

It rushed down the slope and into the valley, vaporizing anything not powerful enough to withstand a wave of spirit magic. Even those enemies with personal shields strong enough to withstand the immediate assault did not escape unscathed and were knocked down like trees in a hurricane.

Focusing her will, she ordered the wave of spirit magic

to shrink in upon itself, forming a heavier, denser substance in the moments before it hit the blood witch.

It was entirely too satisfying to see the witch fly back a good three hundred feet to disappear among the throng of sword carrying enemies. "I think I may need to take up bowling after this."

"Bowling?" Gregory asked along a private link. She sensed as he took out two more of the enemy with barely a pause between kills.

"It's a human game. Never mind. I'll tell you more later," she paused and then added in a mental caress, *"I love you."*

He purred softly in her mind, and then he was focused on the battle once more.

Lillian turned her attention back to the portal spells. Her magic had merged entirely with the spells by now and awaited her command. Good.

"Now it's time to introduce Second Legion," Lillian whispered to herself as she looked upon the fortress city high above.

Reaching out with one hand as magic swirled around the wrist, she sent a command embedded within the magic and flicked it toward the first of the portal spells. She repeated the action twice more, and then all three portals heaved and shuddered as they opened gateways to the Mortal Realm, but instead of where the Battle Goddess had intended, Lillian's magic had redirected the anchors to a specific point deep in the forests east of North Bay.

The sudden opening of the gateways caused a mighty wind to sweep across the valley floor as power rushed from the Magic Realm into the Mortal. And while the enemy soldiers would have been trained to expect the imbalance trying to correct itself, this wasn't how they'd expected it to happen.

Instead of marching into the Mortal Realm with a plentiful amount of magic racing along with them and having time to adjust to the other realm, now they would have to learn to fight with far less magic, while simultaneously having to fight a battle on two fronts.

The portals spun open wider and offered their first view of the Mortal Realm and the massive standing army of Second Legion and the Joined International Task Force.

"Enemies of the Divine Ones," she shouted, magic rising to carry her words across the battlefield so that all might hear, "Meet Second Legion and our other allies. Your demigoddess has overstepped this time and doomed you all."

With war, there would be unavoidable death, but Lillian wasn't without compassion, even for her enemies. "Unlike your goddess and the blood witch, I do not crave death and destruction. If you lay down your weapons and surrender, I shall let you live. My word of honor."

She didn't actually expect any of them to surrender, so wasn't surprised when a roar issued from inside the fortress and a mighty firedrake rose up over the walls and darted toward her.

He was as fierce and beautiful as all his kind. She also knew from reports from Anna, Obsidian, and Gryton that this was Sorac, one of the most formidable of the Battle Goddess's captains. The mighty drake winged his way toward her but was hit and knocked off course by a powerful spear of magic from her protector.

"Love, I can handle a firedrake."

He snorted. "Focus on your job, which is presently the portal spells. I'll keep the riffraff off your tail."

"Fine. I'll return the favor later."

"Sorceress," Greenborrow called and then pointed her to the portal spell and the Legion members already taking flight. "I believe our allies might require your aid."

Hmmm. He was correct. The two enemy battalions were flanking the portal spells. If she didn't do something, there would be a bottleneck as the humans attempted to cross.

"I was never very fond of housework, but I think now is the perfect time for a little sweeping. What say you, Greenborrow?"

The leshii chuckled in delight. "Sweep away, Great Lady."

CHAPTER TWENTY

Anna

From the Earth side of the portal spell, Anna stood shoulder to shoulder with Obsidian. Together they summoned a great shield that would protect Second Legion and the Joint International Task Force long enough for everyone to cross over and get mobilized on the other side.

Anna surveyed the sea of bodies marching on the portal spells. "That looks ugly."

Obsidian snorted at her dry comment but continued to summon magic and funnel it into the shield. She did the same. Though she was still focused on the problem on the other side of the gateway.

"There's no easy route to join First Legion once we're on the other side and not nearly enough room for everyone to deploy. We need to clear an area if we hope to gain a big enough foothold to allow the others to fan out."

Obsidian grinned suddenly. "I believe my sister is already working on that."

He jerked his muzzle in the direction of the eastern slope where Lillian was hovering, a swirling vortex of magic dancing in the air around her.

"Be ready," Lillian said, her voice suddenly in Anna's head. *"I'm going to do a little spring cleaning. It's certainly well past due. However, this is going to use a lot of raw power. I can only afford to do this once."*

Obsidian held his arm up, signaling to the rest of the Second Legion to be ready to fly. Anna relayed the Sorceress's words to Major Resnick, and he passed it up the chain of command. Then Lillian was snapping her wings forward, driving all the raw power she'd just summoned from the Spirit Realm toward the three portals.

"Tell me it's supposed to do that," Major Resnick said as he tensed beside her.

Anna was wondering the same thing, but Obsidian was grinning like an idiot, so everything must be going according to plan.

"Think so," Anna said to Resnick a moment before the magic washed up against the portal spells and then changed directions, racing toward the Battle Goddess's army with renewed force.

The enemy soldiers didn't have time to prepare an adequate defense.

"Ready!" Obsidian called again. Then to Anna, he said. "They'll survive the power since it wasn't forged into battle magic, but they'll be knocked farther down the valley, giving us the opportunity to move into the area newly vacated."

The wave collided with the first line of soldiers, sweeping them back as Obsidian said it would. The power only slowed a little, but the slowing at the front merely drove the power into a taller wave. It continued to grow in height as it rushed down the valley, carrying the right-most flank of the Battle Goddess's army with it.

"Now!" Obsidian roared as he took to the air.

Anna was only a wingbeat behind him.

Thunder rolled through the sky as line after line of gargoyles took to the air with their dryad riders. Anna and Obsidian led the way, crossing the portal swiftly. The heated power of the portal spell was a strange burning pressure against her skin, but then it was over, and she was once again in the Magic Realm.

This time she noticed the flows of power lacked the potency they normally held, and she realized it was because so much of the magic was flowing to Earth.

"Not that now is a good time to ask, but what's all this shit going to do to Earth?"

"The magic?" Obsidian guessed after briefly touching her thoughts. "Likely very little that will be noticeable. The fae that are not here will likely feel the return of magic, but they'll know enough to remain hidden. They won't suddenly rise up and attack the humans."

Obsidian arrowed for the newly cleared ground, winging his way as swiftly as possible to the farthest edge. She kept up with her Rasoren, and when he went vertical in the air, hovering as he called upon his magic, she did the same.

Spreading their arms wide, they released their two powers. Their magic merged and formed the beginning of a wall between them. They continued to feed magic into the spell as swiftly as possible. Once it had enough to hold its form while expanding at the same time, they set it flying toward the enemy soldiers.

Anna and Obsidian followed it, dipping and darting through the air, directing power at the weakest portions until they, too, solidified. The other gargoyles reached their side and added their own magic to the ever-expanding shield wall. Once it was finished, it would provide a barrier for long enough that the rest of the allied forces could make it through.

They just had to protect it long enough that the shield became self-sustaining, drawing power from its environment.

A roar split the air. Jerking her head up from the section she was working on, she scanned the sky. It didn't take long to spot the firedrake winging his way toward them, an angry glint in his eye.

"Think the shield is about to get tested," Anna shouted.

Cursing, Obsidian fed more magic into the shield. "It's not ready for something as powerful as Sorac yet."

"I've got just the thing," Major Resnick shouted as he dropped down from his gargoyle mount and landed next to them. A moment later he was barking something into the radio. He glanced back at him. "Tell your gargoyles to clear the airspace and hit the ground."

Obsidian shouted the order both aloud and in mind speech and every gargoyle in the air dived for the ground. Fifteen seconds later, the first drone flew through the open portal spell. Five more came buzzing shortly behind the first.

Anna could see the firedrake was suspicious of the drones, but he continued on, not knowing the danger. He swiftly learned his painful mistake as the first missile locked onto him. The firedrake roared in pain as the explosion sent him careening wildly through the air.

The great beast crash-landed on the western slope. But with a shake and another loud roar, he launched himself back into the sky.

The next missile streaking toward him was engulfed in his fiery breath before it got near him. The missile's outer casing vaporized in the elemental fire. Three seconds later, the ordnance exploded. It was too far away from the firedrake to do him damage.

Soon the big drake was munching on drones for breakfast, but secretly Anna was glad Sorac wasn't killed. She'd always had a soft spot for him and Vaspara. And after what the succubus had revealed after the assassin spell incident, Anna felt sorry for them.

But the drones served their purpose, and the shield spell had finished maturing while the firedrake was busy. Now a curving dome surrounded the three portal spells in a vast protective shield.

"That's it. We're good. Let's make the Sorceress's sacrifice of power worth it," Obsidian barked.

The remaining members of Second Legion didn't need to be told twice and darted through the portal spell, their wings darkening the sky as they joined Anna and Obsidian and the advanced guard.

On the eastern slope, Anna spotted as First Legion

made their descent, Gregory and Rook already in the air, leading the way.

Behind Anna, the last of Second Legion was swift to make the crossing.

Having a three-mile expanse of open gateway certainly made for a quicker mobilization than the small portal spells they'd been forced to use to travel from Haven to Earth.

The Clan and Coven came next. Whitethorn led the Wild Hunt, his sidhe brethren riding elk and fae horses. Hunting hounds and dire wolves followed close on their hooves. Anna spotted the quarterstaff-wielding form of Gran riding a blazing white fae moose. Beside her raced a dark shifting shadow—Thayn.

Gran raised her staff high above her head, motioning the rest of the Coven to ride. Most of the Coven were mounted on pookas and unicorns, but a few of them had gargoyle mounts as well.

Anna briefly admired the sight they made knowing how much work had gone into building that level of trust and cooperation.

Behind the Coven came the first of the helicopters and armored vehicles.

"Time for Second Legion to earn its keep," Obsidian shouted as he darted toward the shield wall.

She saw the reason why. While the main force of the Battle Goddess's army not in the line of the Sorceress's wave was still gathering itself, one mounted unit of what had to be two thousand riders charged ahead of the rest. The four-legged lizard-like beasts moved much swifter than horses.

"Don't let them reach the shield," Obsidian bellowed.

Anna immediately moved to obey, outdistancing Obsidian in a few wingbeats. The shield was keyed to allow their forces to pass through it, but it became an impenetrable substance if one carrying the taint of darkness or demon blood made the attempt.

But it could only do its job if they provided it with enough power. When they'd come up with the idea, Obsidian had made the calculation using the normal amount of magic present in the Magic Realm, but with the portal spell still open wide, much of the natural magic found in the environment was flowing away into the Mortal Realm.

Obsidian caught up with her. "Don't outrun me next time, unless you want to scare years off my life."

Anna gave him a little mental caress in the way of apology, but it was all she had time for. The mounted riders were almost upon them. Lucky for her and Obsidian, other gargoyles were dropping out of the sky to join them. Truth landed next to them. Meadow rode on his back, a crossbow with a battle magic bolt at the ready.

"Where do you need us?" Truth asked.

"Everywhere," Anna muttered, but Obsidian just told them to stay close. Then they were forging through the shield wall, a line of fierce gargoyles to meet two thousand mounted riders. Not what Anna would call good odds, but soon other gargoyles arrived to help drive off the mounted battalion. The Clan, Coven, and Wild Hunt were swift to join the fray

Now they just had to hold the line.

Holding the line was easier said than done, but through a lot of determination, blood, and sweat they managed. Three hours later, Anna's sword arm was nearly numb, her magic depleted, and she'd lost track of how many she'd killed. Obsidian wasn't much better. Truth and Meadow looked worse than Anna felt.

But they'd kept the enemy off the shield wall long enough for the rest of the Legion and their military allies to make it through the portal spell and take up formations. The rest of the time had been spent fighting their way to First Legion.

"Almost there," Anna said with more cheer than she felt.

More of Second Legion pushed to the front line, galloping past Anna and Obsidian, giving them a much-needed rest.

"Come on," Anna said as she grabbed Obsidian and then tapped Truth with her tail. "Meadow, mount up. We're taking a break."

The words had barely left Anna's lips when magic raced toward them all, the coiling reddish-brown was accompanied by the charnel house scent of old death she'd come to associate with the blood witch.

"Incoming!" Anna shouted the words, but it didn't matter. The gargoyles already had their personal shields up, but the blood magic was strengthened by another power and stabbed right through all their defenses. Anna could only watch helplessly as the gargoyles at the front were mowed down and shredded by the power.

Only Anna's need to save her Rasoren prevented the same thing from happening to him as she drew on lessons taught by the witch. She stole magic from the blood of her fallen comrades and used it to shape another layer of magic—this time blood magic—to her personal shields and then extended them to surround Obsidian, Truth, and Meadow.

The other two weren't aware of what she'd done, but Obsidian knew. While there was a slight horrified look in his eyes, he didn't recoil from her, so she wasn't sure if his look was for what the blood witch had done or for what Anna had been forced to do to protect them. She was reaching for Obsidian's mind to explain, and perhaps beg for his forgiveness, when he shook his head."

"It is done. Dwell no more upon it," Obsidian said, his voice calm and understanding. "You did what you had to do and we'll both continue to do what we must until the witch is dead, and the Battle Goddess is in the Spirit Realm."

A moment later, Gregory dropped out of the sky to land in their midst. He didn't look in their direction as he struck back at the witch, but Anna felt a tendril of the Avatar's magic skim over her and her companions as if he was checking to see if they were unharmed.

The male half of the Avatars called more power than Anna had ever felt before. It crackled in the air, lancing out of the ground and sky to arc across the distance. The ground shook under the repeated impacts.

Clearly, he was trying to hunt down the witch, but by Gregory's curses, she knew he'd lost track of his target in the sea of bodies trying to escape his attack. But by the smoke and ash and burning flesh scent wafting toward them, many of the enemy's front line hadn't escaped unscathed.

Once he'd driven the enemy line back a good three hundred feet, Gregory glanced over his shoulder at them.

"Get ready to order Second Legion back. I'll hold the shield wall while Major Resnick and the Clan and Coven start the second wave of attack." Gregory paused and looked them over a second time. "You look like shit. Report to the healers. We need you in top shape for the final phase of the plan."

Obsidian nodded reluctantly, but Anna still had to drag him away from the front.

"I want the witch's heart," Obsidian growled after he'd given the order for second Legion to move aside for the human military.

As they swiftly moved back, heavy artillery rolled forward to take their place.

"Kick some ass," she told a tank as it opened fire on the enemy army. Then turning her attention back to Obsidian, she reached for him along a private link to speak over explosions and other battle sounds, "We'll talk about who gets to tear out Taryin's heart later after we've been to the healers."

Overhead, a squad of fighter jets screamed past, delivering a more modern version of elemental fire to their enemies.

CHAPTER TWENTY-ONE

Gryton

While the opening salvo hadn't gone as well as it could have, Second Legion and its allies did manage to drive back the enemy and cross over into the Magic Realm. As morning crawled into afternoon, the two Legions fought their way to each other. At last, they formed one large army that stretched from the portal spells to the valley's eastern slope.

For now, the position gave the Divine Ones' army the advantage, the enemy having to battle uphill. But that would soon turn when Light's army needed to cross the valley floor and scale the slopes leading up to the Battle Goddess's fortress.

Of course, Gryton hadn't been permitted to take part in any of the skirmishes that had already happened.

He knew the reasons, but that didn't mean sitting out the fight didn't annoy him. Yet the Avatars were wise in wishing to keep his new abilities a secret until the djinn put in an appearance.

The dragon had advanced far in learning to control his powers, and when djinn and dragon, at last, crossed paths again, the djinn would find his little assassin spells were no longer effective.

Now, if the djinn would just join the fight in a more direct way, Gryton could begin earning his keep. Erika, too, was chomping at the bit while they waited for the djinn.

But while the spirit creature's magic was used to strengthen many of the blood witch's spells, Taryin hadn't let the djinn off his leash yet to take a more direct part in the fighting.

With a growing sense of frustration, Gryton watched as the battle raged throughout the day and into the night. The human military's capabilities had surprised the enemy, driving them back. But even the endless bombardment of bullets, grenades, mortars, missiles, and bombs—Erika had explained to him what each did—could only drive the Battle Goddess's army back so far.

They eventually learned how to create shields that could protect against the various ordnances and how to use magic to attack the modern weapon systems.

There was great loss of life on both sides, and the battle came to a sort of stalemate, where opposing sides paused to lick their wounds, shore up their defenses, and recover their wounded from the battlefield.

It was during this downtime that Gryton was called to meet with his parents.

"Maybe they're finally going to let us fight," Erika muttered from her perch on the unicorn.

His own mount was a much surlier beast. Though the unicorn claimed the pooka was his friend, Gryton doubted the pooka acknowledged any friendships. Or maybe it was just the unicorn's overtures that met with snapping teeth and the occasional kick.

When they reached the impromptu command center, the pooka and unicorn were escorted off in one direction while Gryton and Erika were ushered into a large tent. Inside over two dozen humans did various things on pieces of technology Gryton didn't understand and didn't care to learn.

He ignored the humans and sought out his parents where they stood around a table in the center of the room. Colonel Turner and Major Resnick were there as well. As were Anna, Obsidian, Gran, Thayn, Greenborrow, and Whitethorn. The last two males both glowered at him, but he didn't acknowledge their displeasure at seeing him.

"Our units are driving back the Battle Goddess's army," Major Resnick was saying, "but forging deeper into her territory is going to be more difficult."

Lillian nodded. "We don't actually need to storm her fortress. We just need to make them think that's what we're planning. And then once Lord Draydrak arrives, it won't matter where the Battle Goddess's soldiers are amassed; the battle will be between demigods then. Your only job will be to get your men out of danger and to lock down the enemy army when they try to flee."

"In the meantime, I'm more concerned why we haven't seen more of the blood witch," Anna said as she leaned down and brushed aside several pieces of paper until she exposed a map. "We last saw her here, but nothing has been seen of her since Gregory's assault. Are you sure you didn't manage to kill her?"

Gryton's sire huffed. "If only we were so lucky. But no. She still lives. We all would have felt her death. She's likely working on some nasty bit of spell work. If she doesn't show herself by the end of the day tomorrow, we'll send in Gryton and the Null to flush her out."

"I agree," Lillian said as she gazed upon Gryton. "It's nearly time our enemies beheld our son. However, I think we can lure her out by attacking their temporary base. The spies have seen several of the captains coming and going from the village at the base of the stairs. It's close enough to our front line that one hard push should win us that target. It will have the added benefit of them thinking we're making ready for the final push up the mountain slopes to take the city and confront the demigoddess in her temple."

Colonel Turner glanced at Major Resnick and nodded thoughtfully. Then he started outlining possible attack strategies with the other humans.

Gryton no longer listened, his dragon rising within him at the knowledge he would soon be unleashed to roll across the land like a great, unstoppable wave of destruction.

He glanced back at his mother, wondering if the Sorceress had misjudged him this time. He wasn't at all certain the dragon would listen to reason or even if it would target only the enemy soldiers.

CHAPTER TWENTY-TWO

Anna

With Lillian and Gregory spearheading the push, the enemy's line was broken, and Anna and her Rasoren were able to lead their team into the village. They met little resistance. That was likely because the Avatars had already destroyed or chased out most of the enemy soldiers with their battle magic.

Though, there had still been a few of the enemy hiding among the town's houses as Anna's blood-splattered sword and claws bore testimony.

"I sense humans here," Obsidian said suddenly.

Anna glanced at him, her mind reaching for his thoughts to study what he'd found.

"Hostages," she said darkly. "They were probably planning to use them as human shields."

Obsidian snarled. "The cowardice of such an act…"

She didn't disagree with him as they continued to scout deeper into the town. Obsidian glanced to his right. "Truth and Meadow. Take a unit of legion and human soldiers and scout the town's east side. Thayn. Gran. You take the rest of the legion warriors and search the west side. Anna, River, Darkness, and I will go with Major Resnick's team and take the center."

"Be cautious," River warned the others. "If I were the Battle Goddess or Blood Witch Taryin, I would set traps in case the area was overrun."

Everyone nodded at the dryad's wise words and then set off toward their assigned sections.

They found a few more enemy stragglers. Men and women who had been injured in the initial attack and weren't able to escape with the rest of their brethren. While Anna knew Obsidian would have taken prisoners, the enemy didn't allow themselves to be taken alive.

"Damn it," Anna cursed as the fourth soldier they'd come across died by his own blade. "We could have used him alive."

"They will have been ordered not to allow themselves to be taken alive," Darkness commented. "The Battle Goddess knows we'll try to extract information out of any survivors. She doesn't want us knowing where the blood witch or the djinn are."

Grunting, she admitted River was likely correct. That didn't mean Anna had to like it, though. It would make things so much easier if they knew where the damn witch and djinn were holed up.

A soft brush of magic caressed her mind, and then Thayn was in her thoughts. Obsidian joined them as well.

"Vivien has taken an arrow to her thigh. I fear it might be poisoned," Thayn explained, worry for the woman bleeding across their private link. *"I'm taking her to a healer."*

"Of course. Go," Obsidian ordered, then added as an afterthought. *"Don't fly until you're safely behind our lines. You've been a thorn in the sides of many of our enemies. They'd like to put an arrow in your heart. Don't give them a chance."*

The elder huffed. *"As if I'd allow them the chance."*

But Anna could read his emotions. He would listen to Obsidian. The elder was wise enough to know worry for Gran might distract him.

"Go. And be safe, my mentor." Obsidian's last words were accompanied by warm affection.

A moment later, the elder vanished from their minds, but they could still track his progress as he made his way out of the town.

"Come on," Anna said. "Let's secure the site and free the hostages. Once we know it's safe, we'll allow the rest of the Legion to advance, and then we'll go check on Gran. Lillian is likely already aware and heading toward her."

Obsidian agreed and ordered the group into motion once more.

Shortly, Anna came to a large structure. It might have been the town hall or equivalent. Inside, she could sense the life forces of many humans.

"We found them."

"Yes," Obsidian agreed as he dropped to all fours to sniff around the perimeter of the building. "I don't sense any traps on the stone, but I can smell blood magic."

Anna realized she'd been smelling the same thing, too. But she'd mistaken it for the smell of burnt flesh from the battle magic. The air was full of many unpleasant scents. Obsidian was correct though. When she drew in a deeper breath, she detected the unpleasant odor that was distinct to blood magic.

Obsidian placed his hands on the wall and took out a section of it, intentionally avoiding a door or window. Then he called on his personal shield, layering one layer upon another until it was as dense as she'd ever seen a shield. Anna followed suit.

"Major," Obsidian said, glancing over his shoulder, "stay here with your men. Let Anna, River, and me secure the building. Once we know it's safe, we'll need your help moving the hostages."

Obsidian turned to look at Darkness next. "Father, stay here and be ready to clear us a path if enemies come upon us, and we need to retreat in a hurry."

Major Resnick and Darkness both nodded and then Resnick radioed the plan to the rest of the soldiers in the town who would, in turn, pass the news to the gargoyles and dryads.

Turning from the others, Obsidian leaped through the opening in the wall and Anna followed him in. River came last, one of her swords at the ready.

Soon Anna's sight adjusted to the darkness and she could see the forms of over a hundred people crammed into the room. They were trussed up like cattle in a roping competition at a rodeo.

Obsidian took a step toward the nearest human. He made soothing noises. "Shh. You're safe now. We'll get you out of here and safely away from the battle."

He was leaning down to cut the first person loose when River grabbed his arm.

"No. Get back now."

Obsidian froze for a moment and then jerked back. Anna saw why when he moved a few more steps away from the nearest human, pushing River toward the closest window. A tendril of blood magic rose off the body. More soon joined it and the person—an older woman with long greying hair—made a gagging sound. It was the only noise she was capable of as she choked on her own blood as her veins burst out of her skin and shivered in the air, the blood magic drawing the veins out of the humans' bodies.

"Oh, my fucking God." Anna swallowed as horror tried to physically crawl up her throat.

"Out." Obsidian barked and then shoved her in the direction of the window. Anna didn't hesitate, scrambling out through the broken window after River. She paused to look back and make sure he followed.

Once he was clear, she glimpsed the network of veins spreading across the room and forming a sort of lattice-work. It was already beginning to pulse with power.

"Run," he shouted at the humans.

River already had Resnick by the arm and was dragging him back the way they'd come. The other soldiers followed. Anna and Obsidian ran just behind them. They were only ten feet from the hall of nightmares when Obsidian called out aloud and in mind speech.

"Everyone get as far from the town as you can. It's a trap. Move!"

To the east and west, Anna spotted as gargoyles took to

the air, burdened with more than one rider. Some even carried human soldiers with their clawed feet.

"Should we grab the others and carry them out?" Even as she asked, she knew why Obsidian hadn't already issued the order.

They were too close to what was going to be the epicenter of a magic bomb.

"If we're caught in the air this close, while it likely won't kill us, it might kill my mother and father. It certainly will kill Resnick and his men. But if we get far enough away and build shields low to the ground..."

Anna realized belatedly he was already calling on his magic, summoning more shields into being even as he ran. She began doing the same. They'd only made it about two-thirds of the way out of town when Obsidian gave the order to hit the ground.

River and the human soldiers listened, and then Obsidian was shoving Anna down next to them. His wings snapped out to cover them all instinctively even as he settled his shields around them until a dome covered the small group. Anna lent him her power, adding her strength to his shields.

A moment later, the world flashed white. The ground heaved under them and continued to shake for many seconds. Heat seared them through the shield. A second, even more massive shock wave hit them. Roaring filled her ears.

She briefly wondered if this is what it would feel like the moments before a person was vaporized by a nuclear warhead. Blind and deaf, Anna gripped one of Obsidian's hands harder, and he buried his muzzle in her mane.

"I love you, my Kyrsu," he whispered into her mind. *"And I love you, my Rasoren."*

CHAPTER TWENTY-THREE

Obsidian

His power levels were drained more than he'd ever experienced, and his entire body ached like he'd been slammed around by a rockslide, but if he hurt, Obsidian assumed he had to be alive. Raising his muzzle out of Anna's hair, he looked around.

"Are you all right?" He gave her a little nuzzle.

She moaned and lifted her head. "Yeah. I think so. Can't tell if anything is broken with your heavy ass crushing me, though," she said, defensive sarcasm coming to the fore. It could only mean she'd been terrified.

She wasn't the only one. He'd been certain they were about to die. He'd never felt such force as what that spell had given off.

"Think we know what the blood witch and the djinn

were up to all this time. Is it just me or do you think that spell was designed to kill an Avatar?"

"It isn't just you." Obsidian rolled off her and looked around. Darkness was rising to his feet and flicking his one wing like it didn't want to fold against his back correctly.

Major Resnick moaned and then heaved himself up, spitting grass and blood from a split lip. Obsidian's gaze slid to his mother. Her unmoving form caused a spike of fear, but then his father was gently rolling her over and lifting her into his arms. She moaned and then perhaps realizing where she was, ordered the gargoyle to set her on her feet. Darkness ignored her and drew her closer to his chest.

The rest of the team had survived, but although there were some bumps, bruises, and bleeding ears, lacerated eardrums were a small inconvenience considering what could have happened.

"Everyone up. We can't stay here." Major Resnick's shout got everyone moving.

The devastation stretched far beyond the small village. There wasn't a speck of green growing things or a hint of life in the immediate area. The circle of devastation stretched from just before the portal spells all the way to the first pillar leading up to the blood-red stairway that climbed the slope to the fortress city.

There were no bodies near, but he expected anyone caught in that powerful spell would have been rendered to ash within seconds. Thousands might have died. He didn't yet know the number. Had anyone that had entered the village with him survived?

"God. The witch didn't just kill our people. She must

have killed as many of her own in that strike. She's utterly mad." Anna breathed the last words on a whisper.

And seeing the destruction, he knew his Kyrsu was correct.

"The power from the void has destroyed her mind. We need to get out of here and regroup." Silently he added, *And I need to find Truth, Meadow, Thayn and Gran.*

As they made their way to the edge of the destruction, they saw movement. Legion gargoyles carrying healers onto the battlefield to treat the wounded. He recognized a few of the injured. They were gargoyles who had escaped the town, but who must have later been caught in the outer blast radius.

Thank the Divine Ones some had survived. His friends and mentors may have lived through the attack as well. More gargoyles and healers approached their group and helped to check over the humans. Obsidian waved off the healer who would have attended to him.

"I'm fine." He started to shoo the healer away and then changed his mind. "Have you seen a gargoyle by the name of Truth or a dryad called Meadow?"

The dryad healer shook her head. "No. I'm sorry. But there are many injured and other healers seeing to them."

He nodded. It was a long shot. "What about Adept Thayn or a human woman called Vivien. She often goes by the name Gran."

"Sorry, I'm afraid not."

Obsidian sighed but allowed the healer to do her job.

"Come." Anna took his hand, tugging gently. "We'll keep hunting."

They moved off, following the swath of destruction and

encountering several more injured gargoyles and dryads being seen by healers. There were just as many of the enemy among the wounded. The healers attended to them as well.

"Perhaps, we'll be able to get some intel out of them," Anna said.

He sensed her thoughts and knew she was trying to distract him. They kept searching for a half an hour, Obsidian calling along private links to Thayn, Truth, and Meadow. He was losing hope when he felt a faint reply.

"We're here with a healer," Thayn said, his mind voice sounding far away.

Obsidian moved swiftly in the direction the link guided him. At last, they found Thayn near one of the great portal spells. That explained why he'd been difficult to reach and track. The great spell overshadowed the elders dwindling magic.

"Don't look so worried, young pup. I'm tougher than that, and the healer says Vivien will be fine."

"Of course I'm going to be fine," Gran said with a huff. "It's just an arrow. The healer already neutralized the poison."

Relief washed through Obsidian, and he grinned foolishly. "Don't scare me like that again."

"You scared me, too," Thayn said in a shaky voice. "We couldn't reach you. I knew you were at the center. Thought I'd never see your overly muscled silhouette in the practice ring again."

"Have you seen Truth or Meadow?"

A concerned look flashed across the elder's face before he could school his features. "I saw them as I was leaving with Gran. They would have been a little way behind me when you called out the warning to get out."

The healer looked up from where she was bandaging Gran's leg. "They've only started searching east of here. Start in that direction and call me if you find anything. I'll be there as soon as I'm able."

Obsidian nodded and headed in the direction she pointed. Anna was a substantial presence at his back. They joined their powers to boost their strength and increase the search area. After another fifteen minutes of searching along the great portal spells, a faint answer came to his and Anna's calls.

"Here. We're here." The voice was Truth's, but it was barely above a whisper. Obsidian had only managed to hear it because the wind had died down for the moment. Otherwise, his damaged senses would never have picked up on Truth's weak call.

They rushed to his side and Obsidian froze at what he saw.

Anna did not though and reached out for the healer with her mind. *"Come. We need your aid."*

Truth was curled around a burned and shattered Meadow. If Truth hadn't been holding the female, he wouldn't have recognized her, the damage was so great. Most of her skin was blackened. One arm was missing. So, too, was part of her left leg. But the stumps didn't bleed, cauterized by the very power that had taken the limbs.

By some miracle—or perhaps curse since the wounds must be terribly painful—the dryad still breathed, a wet rattling sound that paused for so long between breaths he thought it was the last, but then she drew another.

Anna knelt next to the pair. When she looked up at him, she gave her head a little shake, and he could see both compassion and grief in her gaze.

Tears wet his cheeks as he came to kneel on Truth's other side. His fellow gargoyle brother had fared no better than the dryad. His wings were missing. He'd likely tried to shelter them both under his wings after his shield had failed, but it hadn't been enough.

"My friend." Obsidian's voice broke on a sob. "A healer is coming. Just hold on a little longer. Can you turn to stone?"

Truth grunted in pain. "No. Beyond that. Just waiting for Meadow now."

Obsidian only then realized his friend was so far gone he wasn't even aware he held Meadow in his arms. He didn't correct his friend.

He'd let him think Meadow was alive and well somewhere in the world, that Truth had been able to protect her.

Anna reached along their link and touched his mind.

"Oh, Obsidian. He knows he's holding Meadow. He's waiting for her to die before he sheds his body and frees his spirit. He's waiting for his love so they can make the journey together."

Another sob built in his throat, understanding too. He would have done the same thing if it were him and Anna burned and broken upon the ground.

"We'll stay with you until the end, Truth," he said at last. "You were my friend. Always so brave and determined. I looked up to you. I wanted to be like you. I'm sorry I wasn't a good enough leader to protect you and Meadow like you deserved."

"Leaders. Hard decisions." Truth's eyes closed, but his mind voice still echoed in Obsidian's thoughts. *"You and Anna, good leaders. Proud to call you my Rasoren and Kyrsu."*

As Obsidian continued to sob over his friend, Truth turned his head and looked at Anna. *"I won wager. You love Obsidian. Pay up. Bragging rights."*

Anna started to cry now, too. "Yes. You won bragging rights. You knew it from the very beginning."

"Make him happy. He deserves love."

"I will do my absolute best. Thank you, Truth. Thank you for being his friend when I wasn't able to be there for him."

"One day we'll see each other... in afterlife. Look me up. Pay debt." He tried to grin but couldn't quite manage it.

Truth blinked his eyes back open and looked blindly toward Obsidian. *"Anna is your one. Don't screw up."*

"I shall heed your words. You have always been wiser than I."

"I am. I ask one other thing."

"Anything, my friend."

"Win. Send Battle Goddess back to be judged."

Truth's eyes drifted closed once more. Then he murmured Meadow's name.

Obsidian glanced down and saw Meadow's chest no longer rose and fell. When he looked back at Truth, he realized the male's no longer did either.

"Safe journey." The words came out in a sob. He collapsed forward over his friends, tears and anguish spilling out of him in a broken-hearted howl.

Anna came around and wrapped him in her arms. They stayed like that until the healer arrived with the other gargoyles. But it was far too late to help his friends. Their spirits were already gone.

In his mind, he could see Truth flying with Meadow in his arms.

"Fly swiftly, my friend and know peace and joy with your Meadow. You've earned it."

After a time, Anna tugged on him and led him away. He followed her blindly, exhausted in mind, body, and spirit. Distantly he heard her talking to others and then a while later, the familiar shape of a tent came into view.

Then Anna was guiding him to a sleeping pallet, and soon her arms were around him once more.

"Obsidian, my Rasoren. I'm here. You're not alone with your grief." Then she drew him closer, her wings settling around him as her tail entwined with his.

"My Anna."

"Yes," she crooned, "I'm here."

And while his pain over Truth and Meadow still burned in his chest, he also took comfort in his Kyrsu.

CHAPTER TWENTY-FOUR

Gryton

"Our side got our asses handed to us yesterday," Erika growled. "That can't happen again."

Gryton wasn't in disagreement about that. "There is one benefit."

She turned to glower at him. "And just what benefit can come from close to two thousand deaths?"

"That spell will have depleted the blood witch a great deal. She won't be at full power again soon. Yet by reports from Resnick and the healers, Anna and Obsidian are nearly fully recovered. We need to strike now."

"We agree," his mother said, joining them. "The witch has ordered the djinn into battle. Are you prepared, my son?"

"Was I not born for this?" he said simply.

Beside him, the Null rolled her eyes. "Translation. Both he and the dragon have been eager to join in the battle. You wouldn't be able to keep him out of it much longer anyway."

Lillian nodded. "Good. We need that. We need every bit of passion, determination, and the will to do what's right. The Divine Ones call for all their allies to rise up and end the madness created by the blood witch and the demigoddess. But we will especially need aid in dealing with Naharnin."

Gryton and the dragon both knew the Avatars shouldn't face the djinn in battle. They wouldn't want to harm their long-time companion. Their hesitation could get them killed.

"When do we engage the enemy again."

"Now. They are already marching upon us."

"Then the dragon has waited long enough." He spread his arms out wide, his power, and the dragon consciousness, rushing to the surface.

He'd startled his mother, but she recovered quickly and stepped back, dragging the Null along with her. She need not have bothered. Neither he nor the dragon would harm either of them.

As he shapeshifted and excess magic expanded outward, he shaped the fire into a screen of flames, smoke, and ash to hide his transformation from watching eyes. His dragon liked the idea of a deception.

"He's such a showman," Erika muttered. But when he held out one forearm, she used it to boost herself up onto his neck. She took a moment more to settle his harness in place. After she'd strapped herself in, she rapped her knuckles against his scales to signal she was ready.

Then he directed the fiery cloud of magic and elemental fire to expand and hide him from his enemies' view.

Before he could get in the air, Gregory darted out of the sky and landed next to the Sorceress.

Gryton glowered at his sire, a curl of steam and flame escaping between his teeth, but he didn't antagonize the male. He was too valuable an ally. The dragon waited until both the Avatars took to the air, and then he merged his thoughts with his Null and soared into the sky.

She welcomed him into her mind with immense joy. He rumbled with happiness that she was once again in his head and on his back, and they conquered the skies. Their emotional bond was always much stronger when he was the dragon than when he wore the form of a man.

"Ever had a gut feeling before?" When he didn't answer, she continued "I just have this feeling we're not going to survive this."

The dragon snorted a denial, but she just patted his neck. "Dying won't be so bad. Imagine being able to explore anywhere in the wide universe. I'll even show you around. Come, let's go take that djinn home with us." She leaned over his shoulder and started to chuckle. "This high, we're almost to Heaven anyway."

An idea flashed across her thoughts like lightning across a night sky, bright and beautiful, but impossible to catch it all before it was gone again.

"Come, let's freak out our enemies by singing as we storm their skies. If nothing else, my singing will have them running in fear, and if this is the last song I ever sing, I know the perfect country tune. Grandad's favorite."

As he flew toward their enemies, Erika started thumping out a rhythm on his shoulder scales. She sang of blue ridged mountains and a river. A few lines later she was belting out about country roads taking her home.

The song and her voice were both strangely pleasing. She continued to sing out the lyrics as he tore through the sky. Amplifying the tune with his magic, he added his own deep crooning tone to the song, and it became a battle prayer as he winged his way closer to the front, a fiery cloud obscuring his form and racing ahead.

CHAPTER TWENTY-FIVE

Sorac

When the blood witch's spell had triggered, a great many warriors on both sides of the battle had lost their lives. Sorac was just glad he'd been assigned to protecting the blood witch. If he hadn't been, he might have been down there and Vaspara with him. And he wasn't at all certain if his lover would have survived the fiery explosion that had shaken the valley floor.

But Vaspara had been with him at the time. A dubious safety to be sure with the blood witch and the djinn near. But Sorac was just glad he hadn't lost his beloved. He wasn't sure what he'd do if he failed her.

Bervicta, too, had survived the explosion, though a large number of the casualties had been from her battalion. The harpy was livid at the waste of life. But he also knew the harpy was fond of all the soldiers under her command. She felt responsible for them.

Sorac admitted he felt much the same about his and Vaspara's battalions. They were their families. And the Battle Goddess and Blood Witch Taryin had started another war. Now they had no choice but to fight and die with the hope they won.

"There is another choice."

Sorac whipped his head around, circling in the sky, his wings flaring as he searched for the djinn. But while the creature's mind voice was powerful enough to sound near, there was no sign of him.

"Another choice?" Sorac asked. *"What choice? The gods have taken all choice away."*

"There are many possible futures. In one, I see only defeat. But there are others." The djinn paused as if he'd lost his line of thought, but then his voice returned. *"Do you know that Lord Death is even now preparing to leave his temple?"*

"What?" Divine Ones be merciful. If Death rode to war, the Lady of Battles would be set free, too. A second cataclysm would be loosed upon the three realms.

"Not this time. Death and the Avatars have another plan. The Divine Ones created a second Avatar pair to receive Lord Draydrak's power. While he surrenders his, the remains of the duality curse will suck away the Battle Goddess's magic as well."

Sorac's heart stuttered in his chest before it started to pound, making his elemental fire burn hotter.

"A second pair of Avatars?" Sorac managed to whisper in his mind.

"Yes. You've met them. They go by the names of Anna and Obsidian. They are young but very powerful."

"Even if it is as you say, the blood witch will not allow that to happen. She'll send you to attack the young Avatars."

"Yes. She even plans to sacrifice me so that my death throes kill this world, taking out both armies. But the Lady of Battles is a demigod. She'll survive."

"You speak madness."

"Look to those you serve for true madness; the type void demons glory in. I only speak of what I've seen in the witch's head." The djinn chuckled then, a cold sound that chilled Sorac's soul. *"The Battle Goddess isn't a match for two sets of Avatars and a mature Gryton. Have you ever seen an elemental dragon, firedrake? You are nothing compared to his power. He will crush you and your succubus love. And once the dragon and the Avatars are finished with the Battle Goddess, they will come for the blood witch, and then the rest of the army."*

"Why are you telling me any of this?"

"Because the blood witch is already weakened from all the spells she's woven. Her hold over me is fraying. I have already unmade the spell she placed over your draklings. Soon I will be free of the witch. Then I will kill everyone except the Avatars, Vaspara, and you. Of course I'll spare the sweet draklings as well."

Sorac wanted to rejoice at the news the death spell holding his draklings hostage was gone, but he doubted the djinn ever acted out of complete benevolence.

"I see your doubt, firedrake. But my bottle has been stored in your old nest site with the draklings. The blood witch couldn't risk the fragile nature of the bottle on a battlefield. So, while I am here pretending to serve and defend the witch, I influenced her into leaving my bottle back with the hatchlings. Free for the taking."

The djinn's power coiled seductively through Sorac's

mind, but even if the firedrake had been able to fight the spirit creature's will, he still wouldn't have.

"You have one chance to rescue your draklings and liberate my bottle. Once you have it, you can command me to reopen the portals to the Mortal Realm and redirect them to a different location. In the chaos, we can escape. Faced with Lord Draydrak's arrival, many of the army will defect along with you both. You and the rest of the refugees can hide in the Mortal Realm, lost in the sea of abundant life there for a short time until we find a new world to make our home with your mate and your draklings."

"You speak to me of the one thing I want more than anything, but if you're wrong..." Sorac hissed softly. *"My draklings. I can't risk them."*

"Then don't take my word for it. The elemental dragon comes. The Avatars beside him. And just behind them, Lord Draydrak will ride. Go to the south-west end of the valley. Cross over the rise. See for yourself."

Then the djinn was gone from Sorac's mind as swiftly as he'd come.

Sorac didn't hesitate and dived, darting toward where he'd left the succubus making more battle magic lances on the grounds of the practice field behind the fortress. He landed hard, sending up a cloud of dust in all directions.

"Vaspara, come to me now!"

She jerked to attention at his words, but her trust in him was absolute, and she ran to his side and vaulted up onto his back without hesitation. Then she settled into place without question. Once he knew she was secure, he launched himself off the fortress's south-facing cliff wall.

"What is it?"

"Gryton comes with his Null. And the djinns says the Avatars fly with him."

"We knew that they'd come soon."

"The djinn says Lord Draydrak will be riding with them."

"What!" Vaspara silenced herself and calmed her body and mind before continuing. *"If Lord Death comes, it will be a cataclysm like the ones of old."*

"Yes. And this one will be worse."

"Worse? How?"

"The djinn says the blood witch is lost to madness. She will sacrifice the djinn to destroy this world, taking out Gryton, his Null, maybe even the Avatars."

"But... but the goddess would be allowing the witch to sacrifice our army."

"Yes."

"She wouldn't do that. Without us..."

"If she is free once more, she won't need us to fight her battles."

"Oh, Divine Ones be merciful." After a few deep breaths, Vaspara was calm once more. *"Could this just be one of the djinn's tricks?"*

"I do not believe so. He wants us to steal his bottle once again and escape with him to the Mortal Realm." Sorac paused, mulling over some of the emotions that had bled into his mind along with the djinn's thoughts. *"He does not want to fight the Avatars or kill their son."*

"We must still confirm this."

"I know. That's why I'm going to go see it for myself." Sorac paused as he realized he had no right to take Vaspara with him if she did not want to go. The blood witch might still have enough power to spare to punish them if she thought

they were trying to escape. *"If you want to stay here, I understand."*

"I'm going with you, you great idiotic lizard, but we need to inform our battalions first."

"Of course. I was just waiting until I knew if you wished to come."

Then he reached out for the minds of his and Vaspara's battalions, swiftly informing them that they were scouting for a new danger Sorac sensed coming. Then curling a wingtip, he set a course for the distant south-west end of the valley.

Below him, there was a ripple of movement as his and Vaspara's battalions saluted them as he flew overhead.

He crossed the length of the valley floor swiftly, but he didn't need to go more than half the distance to confirm the djinn's words.

A pillar of fire and power was rising up into the sky, stretching from mountain peak to mountain peak. The shape wasn't that of a dragon, but Sorac sensed this was a fire elemental. It had to be Gryton.

As the cloud stretched wider, it began to move, streaking toward them.

Sorac had seen enough to confirm the djinn's words. He twisted in the air, circling back around. He was still turning when he saw the Avatars take to the air on either side of the burning storm.

As the valley opened up into deep sweeping slopes, the fiery cloud shifted and flowed down the slope, leaving Sorac a view of a four-armed, four-legged, winged monster flying some distance behind the cloud. The demigod was swiftly catching up to the Avatars and their storm-cloud son.

Sorac roared a warning to his soldiers, but the elemental dragon must have mistaken it for a challenge, for the beast at last shed its storm cover. As the monstrous molten bronze and gold beast with wings the width of the valley showed itself, it roared out its own challenge.

It was only then that Sorac realized there was a rider on the beast's back, and she was singing like she was on a pleasure flight, not winging her way closer to war.

The Null's absolute disregard for the seriousness of what was about to happen terrified Sorac more than anything else he'd seen or heard.

As the dragon drew closer, Sorac could make out the words of the Null's song. She was singing about going home. And by the djinn's own words, she was one of the ancient First Wave. Her home was the Spirit Realm, and she was singing about returning there. Great goddess. She planned to take them all with her.

Sorac screamed again and winged his way back toward the city fortress. When he was once again over his soldiers, he bellowed out another warning.

"We've been betrayed. Lord Death comes. The blood witch and the Battle Goddess have betrayed us. They plan to destroy us all. Retreat. Save yourselves!" He opened his mind to all the battalions and blasted them with everything the djinn had said and what Sorac had just confirmed with his discovery.

His duty to his soldiers fulfilled, Sorac retreated from the firestorm giving chase and desperately winged his way back to the fortress. He had to rescue his draklings and get the djinn's bottle. It was the only way to stop the blood witch from forcing the djinn to sacrifice himself.

"Fly, my love. Fly!" Vaspara called encouragement, and he flew faster than he ever had before.

Moments later, he was arrowing down into the city where he landed and stormed the fortress, uncaring of what happened to anyone foolish enough to get between a firedrake and his draklings.

CHAPTER TWENTY-SIX

Bervicta

"My captain. What are your orders?" Bervicta's second-in-command asked.

"To the void with both the blood witch and the Battle Goddess," Bervicta bellowed, then she looked her Second in the eye. "Gather the battalion. I don't know about you, but when Sorac flees in terror, it's a signal to get your ass in motion and follow him."

"My Captain?"

"Gryton knew the Battle Goddess would lose. Anna and Shadowlight knew. Now Sorac and Vaspara are leaving. Do you want to stay and die? Or would you prefer to follow the other two captains? Those two are survivors. They'll have an escape plan. I plan on going with them."

"But the Battle Goddess..."

"You heard Sorac. He's the most honest person I know. We've been betrayed by the very one we serve. Time to cut our losses and save our backsides."

Bervicta took to the air. She knew where Sorac was headed, and she'd help him and Vaspara battle their way to the draklings. There were worse ways to die than at the side of a friend.

CHAPTER TWENTY-SEVEN

Anna

"*D*id that really just happen?" Anna asked as she watched Sorac tell the entire lot of the Battle Goddess's army to retreat.

"Yes," Obsidian said, sounding only slightly less surprised than she felt. "He was always a smart one, seeing the truth of things."

The Sorceress joined them, dipping lower to fly at Anna's right wingtip. "That was some of Naharnin's work. He has been whispering some truths into that firedrake's ear, I would bet."

Anna merely nodded.

Whatever the source, it was a great boon. The Battle Goddess's army was in disarray with about half of the battalions marching forward to meet the Divine Ones' army, and the other half in a disorganized shuffle, trying to decide what to do now that half their leadership had just defected. She imagined they would attempt to retreat and escape.

While they had nowhere to go, the added chaos would only help Anna's side.

The only one that seemed disappointed was the dragon. He was clearly spoiling for a fight and thought some of his victims were getting away.

But Anna had other concerns beside what the elemental dragon might think. She glanced at Obsidian for what was probably the fifth time.

"I'm fine," he rumbled softly into her mind.

He wasn't, of course, not after losing two of his oldest friends. Anna worried for him. Physically, the healers had helped to restore him bodily, and his magic reserves were back up to what they'd been before, but his emotions...

That kind of trauma couldn't simply be mended away by the healers.

He glanced at her again. *"I will be fine, my Kyrsu. While my grief over my friends is very vivid, and the thought of never seeing Truth again in this life isn't something I can fully accept, I will not fail you like I did them."*

"Obsidian, you didn't fail them. It's war. People die. There was nothing you could have done to save them."

"I will not let the enemy have you. I..." he trailed off, and she felt his thoughts scatter, unable to face the thought of losing her like he had Truth and Meadow. *"As much as the loss of my friends pains me, I couldn't go on without you."*

"Of course you would."

"Oh Anna, the link that binds us; I'm not sure if we would

survive the other's death. And if you died before me, I would gladly surrender my life to follow you into the afterlife."

Anna hadn't even thought of what one of their deaths would do to the other. She wouldn't lie to herself, the thought of losing him terrified her and had been the fuel for her nightmares the last few nights. Now that he'd mention they might not survive each other's deaths, it brought a morbid kind of relief.

But she couldn't tell him that. Instead she reached for his mind once more. *"Good partners don't die on each other. They live for each other. But in battle, nothing is certain. If we do meet our end, promise me we'll do it shoulder to shoulder."*

"That I can promise," he rumbled softly in her mind, his thoughts full of love and determination.

Then they were nearly upon the enemy army, and there was no time for anything except the present.

The elemental dragon issued another of his deep roaring challenges. A moment later, Anna saw why as a bronze-toned being with flaming tattoos rose into the air five hundred feet ahead. Molten power swirled and danced in the air around him, and suddenly he was growing in size until the djinn was every bit as large as either the Lord of the Underworld or the Lady of Battles.

But the dragon was larger, and if Anna wasn't mistaken, more enraged.

Screaming challenges, the fire elemental dived, arrowing toward the djinn.

CHAPTER TWENTY-EIGHT

Erika

Erika hollered encouragements to her dragon mount. They were both going to need every bit of encouragement for the coming fight. Even from across the valley, she'd been able to sense just how powerful the djinn was. He was equal to one of the Avatars easily. And he'd only grown scarier the closer they got.

But Gryton was born of the Avatars and was a demigod in his own right.

And the dragon had something the djinn didn't—her, the mother of all Nulls.

"Come on, motherfucker! Give us your best!"

Then the dragon was swinging all four of his legs into position, talons poised to rend. The djinn blasted them with a wave of magic, but it never hit, Erika having reached out with her talent and sucked the magic into herself.

"Nice try!" Then she reached farther, digging mental claws into the djinn's swirling magic.

He sensed the danger and propelled himself away from them and up onto the valley's western slope, climbing higher until he was perched up on the ridge.

Erika narrowed her eyes at him. "Oh no, you don't. You're not getting away."

But as soon as Gryton turned and pursued, Erika realized the djinn's plan. As much as her dragon was a magical beast, he still had form and mass, still had a body and was limited in this form. He had to fight his way up the steep slope, battling the wind currents that blew over the mountain's ridge.

And as she watched, the djinn fed more power into that breeze until it turned into a howling, many-toothed force. Snow and ice shards rained down upon them.

She was lucky. Sort of. As soon as the frozen water hit the dragon's fiery shields, most of it turned to vapor and hit them as a thick mist.

"Damn it! Is the bastard trying to drown us?" Erika changed tactics, no longer trying to drain the djinn. He was too powerful to do so quickly, if at all. She switched to stealing the magic from his spells instead.

Her dragon made headway and then roared another challenge. This time a stream of molten magic issued from between his jaws. The fire struck the ice and snow just below the djinn. Erika thought the dragon had missed until the snowpack on the mountain peak began to crumble. While some of it avalanched down the mountainside, a vast majority of it vaporized at the contact with his elemental fire.

Magic-laced steam rose up in front of the djinn, forming a foggy sort of barrier. Erika didn't understand the purpose until the dragon winged his way to the top and then swung his talons forward with another screamed challenge.

This time the djinn was blinded by the attack and didn't move fast enough to avoid Gryton's lightning-fast strike. The two came together with a sound like thunder rolling off the hills. Erika was nearly dislodged from the dragon's back, but her harness held.

She clawed at Gryton's scales as he went into a barrel roll trying to avoid the djinn's strikes as they battled in the air, trying to gain mastery over each other.

The djinn was older and slyer, though. He attacked the dragon's wings, knowing a grounded opponent would be much easier to destroy.

But when the djinn attacked with claws of power intent on shredding the dragon's wing membranes, the spirit creature's claws dissolved as the magic forming them was sucked away.

"Oops! Wasn't expecting that, were you jackass?" she shouted overtop of the roar of fire and the thunder of the dragon's wings.

Trying a new tactic, she extended her Null's abilities to surround her dragon like a set of magic-absorbing armor. Most of the djinn's strikes didn't penetrate deeply enough to threaten her dragon.

Or at least for now, until she had glutted herself on magic and reached her upper limit. She still had one. But thanks to the last few days of constant practice, she'd stretched her limits, and the upper threshold of how much power she could consume was now more than triple what it had been only a few days ago. She also had the advantage of being able to radiate magic back into her dragon partner, making him stronger.

But the djinn wasn't an easy opponent to fight. For one, he didn't seem to feel pain. No matter how many strikes her dragon landed, the djinn wasn't hampered by his injuries. For that matter, the djinn appeared to absorb the damage and regenerate.

"Are we even making a dent?"

"Yes," the dragon hissed. "Just not enough of one. Maybe this will do it."

Then her dragon struck.

Like a giant game of pool, the force of Gryton's strike drove the djinn downward at ballistic speeds. The impact leveled part of a mountain, and when the dust cleared enough to see, she spotted the djinn.

The sharpest point of the mountain range poked up through his chest.

"I don't care if you're a two billion-year-old djinn. That's got to hurt like a son of a bitch."

But the djinn didn't struggle to free himself as she'd thought, highlighting the fact they weren't fighting a flesh and blood opponent. Power rose up out of the djinn's body, a great shimmering wave of golden magic. As she watched, his form shimmered, shrinking in size. That could only mean he was putting a lot of himself into his next attack.

"Shit! Look out!"

Gryton darted to the side a moment before the djinn

launched the wave of raw power at them. Erika tried to absorb as much of it as possible, but there was just too much moving too quickly.

The dragon screamed and wheeled in the air, but the power's path shifted with the dragon, and he wasn't able to escape in time. The power collided with them, slamming the dragon into the side of the opposite mountain.

Erika was tossed forward into the dragon's neck. Her arms only absorbed a little of the impact, and her nose and right cheek took the brunt.

There was a sickening wet crunch and then a stabbing pain. Moments later, blood gushed down her face. By the pain, she'd just broken her nose. But she had bigger concerns as all around her the dragon's elemental fire erupted as he fought his own magic.

Erika was reminded of the djinn's first assassin spell. But the dragon was more in control than Gryton had been back then, and he managed to hold his form. Not that it aided them much. The impact had been so great, it had buried his lower body partway in the mountainside.

"Fuck!" she muttered as air and blood bubbled out her nose. She made an aborted attempt to touch it and then changed her mind.

Then she looked beyond her dragon's flapping wings and snaking neck and discovered he was buried nearly up to his neck.

"Shit. How badly are you hurt?"

"Only my pride," the big beast said sounding very much like the Gryton of old. Then the dragon dispensed with words and settled for hisses and snarls as he struggled to extract himself from the side of the mountain.

Erika swiveled her head to get a look at what the djinn was doing while her dragon was stuck. She quickly found the djinn. He was still on the opposite side of the valley, picking himself up off the mountain peaks. Just like his earlier injuries, these new one simply shimmered and closed over, repairing the djinn like he hadn't just been impaled on the jagged teeth of a mountain.

Though there was one difference. She hadn't been mistaken. The djinn was about twenty feet shorter than he'd been before. Erika was just about to tell her dragon the good news when the djinn turned his back on them and began pouring more of his power into the mountain he'd recently been impaled upon.

Magic raced along the cliffs, slopes, and crevasses of the mountain. Large pieces sheared off. The ground began to shake as if by an earthquake.

"I don't know what the djinn is doing, but I don't think I like it!"

Shortly the djinn rose to hover above the mountain and then his muscular shoulders shifted and strained as if he was about to...

"Fuck! I think he's going to toss a mountain at us!"

The longer she watched, the more certain she was that he planned to entomb both her and her dragon between two mountains. Gryton might survive that, but she doubted even the most powerful of Nulls could survive such a thing.

"This is not how I envisioned returning to the Spirit Realm."

Under her, the dragon bucked and clawed and flapped his wings in a renewed effort to free himself, but his fire magic had melted the rock around them, and he couldn't get traction.

And as his fire magic melted more and more of the mountainside, the heat rolling up off the molten rock became even more unpleasant until it was nearly unbearable.

"Hot. Hey there, Dragon, it's getting really hot." She tucked her arms and legs closer to her torso. It helped a little. The scales underneath her were still relatively cool. Either the dragon was protecting her, or her Null's ability had sensed a threat and had kicked in, draining away the heat.

Gryton thrashed and beat his wings, levering his neck and shoulders away from the mountainside. She chanced a glance over her shoulder again. The djinn was still working on lifting a mountain. But as she watched, large fissures formed two-thirds of the way down the slope. "Fuckity. Fuck. Fuck. He's lifting the mountain!"

With a mighty heave, the dragon extracted his front end and beat his wings harder until slowly more of his body emerged from the molten rock. Erika cast a terror-filled glance over her shoulder.

The djinn hurtled the mass of mountain at them.

Closing her eyes, she pressed both palms against the dragon's scales and calmed her mind. "You are the most magnificent creature a girl could ever ask for. Thank you for coming into my life. It was an honor flying with you."

With a mighty roar that shook the mountain, her dragon pulled himself free of the sucking molten rock and shot into the air. He didn't slow, darting up into the sky so swiftly the temperature plummeted. The molten rock sticking to him cooled and fell away.

Higher and higher, he flew, until the air grew thin. Then he rolled and hung weightless for a moment.

Erika grew light-headed even as she laughed with joy.

"You really are the most magnificent of creatures!"

Then the moment of weightlessness was over, and suddenly a force was threatening to pull her from his back, but the sturdy leather harness held her in place. He descended even faster than he'd shot up into the air. Soon the valley was growing larger once more. She spotted the djinn looking up at them.

He launched more power, but it had no effect, her dragon just slicing through it like it wasn't there. The dragon swung his claws forward. Three seconds later, he struck the djinn. The impact of the two opposing magics created a shockwave, knocking her dragon back two hundred feet before his wings were able to compensate. Below them, the concussion knocked the two armies off their feet. The djinn, lacking wings, flew backward until he smashed into the fortress city.

It wasn't until a tall, ethereal giantess had to sidestep the djinn that Erika realized the other factions were making war upon each other even as she and her dragon fought the djinn.

The Lady of Battles was free from her temple prison. She wore a black breastplate, carried a shield nearly as tall as she was, and wielded a very long sword. Power rippled in the air as she moved, and Erika somehow knew she was drawing power from the other battles, using it to strengthen herself.

"She's like a twisted sort of Null," she mused, coming to understand the Battle Goddess's power for the first time.

"Yes. She draws power from war and aggression. It is her nature. And we must help the other Avatars and her twin to defeat that great power."

Erika raised her fist into the air. "Bring. It. Bitch!"

CHAPTER TWENTY-NINE

Obsidian

The spectacle of watching dragon and djinn battle it out was enough of a distraction that many did not see the demigoddess until she'd begun to descend the dark red stairway leading down from the fortress city. Obsidian had been among the number focused upon the elemental dragon and the djinn.

As much as he'd disliked Gryton, he could only hope that the dragon won the fight. They needed the djinn out of the way for what was to come next.

Turning his attention fully to the Lady of Battles, Obsidian noticed for the first time that she was herding many warriors ahead of her. Power cracked at them like whips, forcing them to flee before her or die. Her plan was clear. She would force them into battle, which would only make her even stronger. And if they refused to fight, she'd kill them with her lightning-like power.

Obsidian already knew the warriors would fight. It was what they'd been trained for. A spike of regret flowed through him. Sorac and Vaspara were probably already dead. The Battle Goddess would not have shown them leniency for what the firedrake had tried to do to save those under his command.

Anna's thoughts brushed his. *"We'll avenge them as well."*

Yes, they would.

Lillian and Gregory soared past him, spiraling down to the ground to land at the head of the army. Obsidian and Anna dropped out of the sky to join them.

"We need to engage the Battle Goddess now before she can force the two sides into a fight," Lillian said. "My other half and I will distract the demigoddess while Draydrak begins the transfer of power."

Obsidian nodded at his older sister. "We will join the fight as soon as we're able."

"Be safe, little brother," she called over her shoulder. Then she began to run forward, magic already snapping around her. Gregory ran close beside her, his equally formidable magic racing ahead of them both, forming a lance that he sent speeding toward the Battle Goddess.

The sound of large hooves crunching on the rocky ground announced Lord Draydrak's approach. "It is time. Are you ready to fulfill your purpose, young Avatar?"

Obsidian pushed aside the nervous shiver that wanted to run down his back and into his wings. But there was no time for fear. This is what he'd been born for; what he'd trained for. If they had any hope of finally defeating a demigoddess who could not die, this was the only way.

Warm, strong fingers closed around his. He tilted his head to study his Kyrsu.

Anna, with her muscular body that still possessed soft curves, her broad wings, her beautiful dark skin, and her lovely eyes shining with determination and love.

She noticed his scrutiny. "We got this. We're a team, remember?"

He huffed in agreement and then looked toward Lord Draydrak. "I am ready."

"Good, if this works, you shall become death." Draydrak paused to look to Anna. "And you shall become war."

Anna's thoughts touched Obsidian's mind. *I'm not sure what part I like less—the 'you shall become death' part or 'if this works' bit.*

Lord Draydrak took one of his swords and sliced a long cut down the center of his gargoyle torso. When he lowered the sword, power continued to pour down his chest. The wound didn't seem to pain the demigod. He gathered up the power and wove it into tendrils until he had a length of magical rope held between two of his hands.

With a flick of his wrist, he tossed one end, and it adhered to the wound and the rope glowed brighter with power. Then he took the other end and handed it to Obsidian.

Gazing down at the ghostly filaments waving in the air, Obsidian drew a deep calming breath and then brought the umbilical up to his chest. When it latched on, pain lanced through his core, deep enough he thought it cut into his soul. A shudder traveled down his spine, wings, and tail. Anna's fingers tightened around his.

"We've got this," he murmured back at her a moment before the power of death came rushing into him. At that moment he felt every death that was occurring the universe over, every soul beginning its journey into the Spirit Realm. Obsidian collapsed to his knees with a gasp.

"It will be over soon," Draydrak said, his voice loud in Obsidian's mind. *"And you will not have to learn to wield my power. You are only a vessel. A source for my swords to draw power from. They will attend to what needs doing. After all, they too have souls and consciousness. Do not be afraid if you should hear their voices. They will not harm you. If they become too loud, you can command them to silence, and they will remain so unless they determine that there is some danger to the souls of the universe that needs your attention."*

"I understand."

"Good. Then relax as much as you are able."

Obsidian nodded and allowed Draydrak to continue his work. He had no sense of time as Lord Death poured more and more of his power into him. Though he knew the battle still raged on around them. Yet at no point did Anna's fingers ever leave his.

"There," Draydrak said as he stepped back, allowing the sun to once again touch Obsidian's skin.

Its warmth was welcome. Inside he burned with power, and yet his soul felt chilled.

"That is the spirit magic you feel. In time, you'll grow accustomed to it."

Looking down, Obsidian expected to see the magical rope still adhered to his chest since he still felt magic flowing into him from Draydrak, but there was no sign of the enchanted umbilical cord.

"It is no longer needed," Draydrak explained. "You now host enough of my power that the rest will flow to you naturally."

"What about me?" Anna asked the same thing Obsidian had been thinking. "What do I have to do to take your twin's power?"

"Not die." Draydrak laughed and then sobered a moment later. "Forgive me. That joke was in poor taste. As soon as my twin feels the first pull upon her magic, she will understand what we try to do. She will retaliate most fiercely."

"Hence, the 'not die' part, I take it?"

"Yes. The only way she can win is if she kills you or Obsidian. The Avatars and I will do all in our power to prevent that from happening. You have my word." Then Lord Draydrak drew another of his swords and made a second slash on his chest. Soon he was weaving together another rope of power. When he was finished, he held out the end to Anna like he had with Obsidian.

Anna only shrugged and pressed the wiggling tendrils of power to her breast. Then she gasped out a startled oath. Obsidian squeezed her hand. It was important that she know he was here for her like she'd been for him. As she shivered and shook under the powerful onslaught, he continued to croon to her.

Then at last with a little shudder, she looked up and blinked at him.

"Hell. That was a bit of something, wasn't it?"

He nodded his agreement. While she was patting her

chest where the ropelike tendrils had been, he glanced up at their surroundings. Light's army had moved past them to engage the enemy.

The Avatars were battling the Battle Goddess.

Suddenly there was a screech from the distant battlefront. The Lady of Battles raised a hand toward them, screaming something incoherent. Before the echo had died away, she was launching a new attack aimed at Anna.

Lord Draydrak blocked it with one of his swords and then glanced down at Anna. "It seems my sister has discovered my little plan."

"I'd say so by the rage in that scream. She sounded pissed."

"Come. The closer you are, the faster you'll be able to draw magic away from her."

Anna and Obsidian nodded and took to the air.

They were nearing the line of fighting between the two armies when Blood Witch Taryin's voice slashed across the distance, harsh and demanding as she ordered the djinn to destroy Anna and Obsidian.

There was a rippling in the power surrounding the djinn, and Lord Draydrak stepped between them and the other spirit creature. But the djinn merely smiled at them and then turned back to the witch.

"No," he said as he rose up into the air and waved a hand at the dormant portal spells. Once the portal spells flashed active, he turned back to the witch. "I no longer serve you. I have a new master."

He waved his hand at the fortress city. A firedrake and his two riders could be seen winging swiftly toward the open portal.

Obsidian felt a spark of joy at the sight of fourteen tiny draklings lodged between the firedrake's spine ridges. They were within ten wingbeats of the portal when Vaspara held up the bottle.

There was a moment of panic when both armies stirred uneasily, fearing she was going to smash the bottle and unleash the djinn to annihilate this world, but she merely called to it, and the spirit creature dissolved into pure light and raced after them.

The firedrake darted low, breathing fire at the Legion soldiers guarding the portal gates. The drake dived a second and third time until the gargoyles had to scatter or burn as their shields failed.

In the moments between heartbeats, the firedrake and his passengers vanished through the portal.

Eerie silence spread through both armies. Then there was a stirring in the ranks of the Battle Goddess's army. A moment later three of the battalions that had pulled back from the fighting now saw another possibility and charged toward the gateway. The Legion members scattered by the firedrake's earlier attack weren't able to rally in time to hold back the sudden flood of enemy soldiers all coming at them at once. While many of the battalion members died, many hundreds made it through the portal.

Beside him, Anna cursed. "Are they about to arrive on Earth?"

"I am uncertain. I felt the djinn's power working upon the portal spell. It's possible he changed the destination point."

CHAPTER THIRTY

Gregory

The battle was nearing an end. Gregory could feel it in his soul. Many had lost their lives, but the Light would win the day. And if there were mercy in the universe, this would bring about a lasting peace.

But before that could happen, the Battle Goddess needed to die, and it was clear he wouldn't be able to accomplish that in this flesh and blood form.

"I will keep her busy while you shed your corporeal form," Draydrak told Gregory.

He nodded his thanks to the demigod as the male galloped past, bringing his swords into play.

The two demigods came together in a clash of shield and sword. By rights, Draydrak's four swords to the Battle Goddess's one should have given him a great advantage, but his opponent was War, so it came as no surprise that the Lady of Battles held her own against her four-armed opponent.

But she would be no match for the Avatar.

Closing his eyes, Gregory shed his gargoyle body and burst free to race up into the sky. His form expanded, his magic shimmering pure and cold and powerful until, once again, he was an ageless primordial being from the beginning of the universe.

"Your reign of war is over," he told the Lady of Battles as he grabbed her by the shoulders and dragged her toward the vortex his Sorceress was opening in the sky above them. The cold, pure power of the Spirit Realm rushed down to him from the rip in the Veil Between the Realms.

He was almost within touching distance of the vortex when his sudden momentum came to a jarring halt. He glanced down at his prey only to see ropes of blood magic trailing from her body like chains. The corrupted magic dragged upon the Battle Goddess harder, making her scream and thrash. The twisted power began dragging him down with her.

His will was greater than a witch's though, and he tugged harder, regaining the few feet of height he'd lost. But more of the tainted magic shot out from deep inside the Battle Goddess's temple and attempted to drag her back to the ground.

A moment later, the Lord of the Underworld took to the air and was slashing at the coiling tendrils with his swords. But for each one he severed, three more grew out of the severed end.

Gregory growled at the sight, hating blood witches.

This one needed to die. Unfortunately, he had his hands full with the struggling demigoddess. She was drawing power from the blood magic and her strength was returning.

He cursed all blood witches to the void. Once he was finished here, he'd seek out the witch and shred her soul.

But then his other half was there, rising up from the ground, surrounded by shimmering power even though she was still clothed in a flesh and blood body. It would be easier for her to fight in her natural form, but he knew why she didn't sacrifice her body yet. She wouldn't unless there was no other choice.

But with Lillian's aid slicing through the blood magic tendrils, hoisting the Battle Goddess's essence toward the Spirit Realm grew easier, and with a mighty beating of his vast wings, and aided by Lord Draydrak, he dragged the demigoddess closer to the rip in the Veil Between the Realms.

He didn't see the lance of tainted blood magic until it pierced the substance of one of his wings. Roaring in pain, he struck back at the witch, but the distraction allowed the Battle Goddess to renew her fighting. She almost slipped free of his hold.

"No, you don't, you arrogant little neophyte."

CHAPTER THIRTY-ONE

Lillian

There was no other option open to her. Her other half needed her help. The Battle Goddess was putting up too much of a fight, and with the blood witch's aid, they were once again dragging the male half of the Avatar soul back down with them. Lord Draydrak was slashing and striking and stomping at the deathless, vine-like spell that continued to grow out of the fortress city. But his magic wasn't having much success destroying something that wasn't really alive. Draydrak couldn't die; he would be fine. But Lillian knew it was a delicate and dangerous time for her other half.

He was vulnerable until she joined him in the Spirit Realm, and they mended their soul, becoming a single being once more. Only then would they have the strength needed to defeat their enemies.

But to do that she must shed this body. When it died, so too would so many of her dreams. Her mind scrounged for a way to save the life of her unborn child.

Yes, the Avatars would die. Again. The facts were irrefutable. Their soul had no control over the most fundamental laws controlling it. But with their death, their unborn child would perish. The thought of that sparked great anguish within her.

There had to be a way.

Then in a moment between seconds, one glimmer of hope presented itself. Her other half saw it as well. Was that why he hadn't incinerated his body when his powerful soul freed itself?

Gripping that slim hope, the Sorceress landed and shifted back to her dryad form. She swiftly began weaving a powerful preservation spell over her body. Finishing her spell in such haste, she knew it was not her greatest work, but it was all she had time for.

The blood witch was triggering more spells. One blasted out from somewhere within the fortress city, racing down the length of the vines. Lillian caught a taste of its essence and immediately knew its purpose. It was designed to attack the Veil Between the Realms and it would use Lillian's vortex if she didn't stop it.

But the witch's target wasn't to invade the Mortal or Spirit Realms. This spell would open a gateway into the void, allowing the true demons back into the universe.

That couldn't be allowed to happen.

But only the single being known as the Avatar could

prevent the nightmare scenario of the blood spell tearing apart the Veil.

"My son," she called out to the dragon, *"I must leave you to protect the Veil and contain the witch until after your father and I have dragged the Battle Goddess into the Spirit Realm, and I've had a chance to heal the rift. Be strong and quick, my beautiful one. And be safe. Goodbye."*

She had no other choice. The universe needed the Avatar. She only hoped she didn't have to sacrifice either of her children to save it.

"Divine Ones, please protect my children."

Then the Sorceress shed her flesh and blood body and rose into the sky, her power burning around her as she chased after her other half and helped him drag the Lady of Battles into the Spirit Realm.

CHAPTER THIRTY-TWO

Anna

She could only watch as the Sorceress sacrificed herself to aid the male half of the Avatars to wrestle the Battle Bitch into the next life. If Anna could have done something to help, she would have. But as it was, she could already feel her body's need to rest, and if she wasn't mistaken, it was already preparing to turn to stone.

She glanced toward her Rasoren. He didn't look much better.

"I need to get to my sister's body to stand guard. She might yet return," Obsidian said.

Anna wanted to reassure him, tell him Lillian would return to them, but this felt different than the time

Gregory had shed his mortal body to battle Gryton's dragon the first time the beast had appeared.

Oh, her poor Obsidian. Had he just witnessed the death of his sister? There had already been so many deaths. Why did he have to lose everyone he loved?

But she would go with him and guard the body of his sister. It was the least she could do.

"Come." She held out her hand as she took to the air.

Obsidian was slow to follow, and she realized he was having trouble getting his big body into the air. She slowed her pace to match his, staying wingtip to wingtip until they reach the spot where they'd seen Lillian land to shed her body.

To her surprise, others were already there when they reached the spot. Anna recognized Gran and Thayn first. Vivien was bent over her granddaughter, working to shore up the spells protecting her body.

Gran looked up at their approach. "Lillian's soul is gone, but the Sorceress did something to protect the body and keep it alive. And Gregory is stone, not dead. That must mean they will try to return. But they can only return if they have bodies to return to. Resnick and a company of human, legion, and fae soldiers are guarding Gregory, so he's safe for now."

Anna nodded in acknowledgment of Gran's words. As long as they could protect the Avatars' mortal bodies, there was still hope they'd return to life.

Beside them, the unicorn and the pooka were standing guard. Both equines looked like they'd been to hell and back. The pooka was limping, a deep gash marring his flank. The unicorn looked even worse, covered in cuts and bruises and burns. His horn had been snapped off three inches from his skull.

A shadow flashed across the ground, and Anna instinctively had her sword out, but the gargoyle's silhouette was familiar. Darkness came in for a landing a moment later. River leaped off his back and was running toward Lillian before the gargoyle had even touched down completely.

There were other legion gargoyles arriving with them, but they landed in a defensive line just below the brow of the mountain ledge. A moment later, Anna saw why. Hundreds of enemy soldiers were climbing the slope toward them. She didn't know if they merely sought to escape or if they were actively hunting the Sorceress to desecrate her body in an act of vengeance.

"We gotta move!" Anna shouted.

Obsidian went to Lillian's other side. "I can carry her."

"No." Gran held out a hand to stop him. "She can't be moved. The preservation spell is healing the body. It's anchored to the ground around it. If you sever that, it will unmake the spell. Without the Sorceress here to revive the body, I don't know what will happen. Lillian might die for good."

Gran wiped at her tears. "I don't know where Jason or Greenborrow or Whitethorn are, but I'm not losing any more of my family or friends if I can help it."

"If we can't move her," Anna barked, new determination taking hold of her spirit, "then we damn well will protect it here."

The sky overhead suddenly darkened, and the great elemental dragon came in for a landing downslope. Anna didn't miss how he put himself between his mother's body and the enemy soldiers making their way up the slope.

Erika swiftly unhooked herself from her harness and slid down the dragon's neck. In moments, she was running to join Anna. "I'm in a radiating mode. Gryton can't drink any more of the power. Anyone here need a recharge before we go kick the blood witch's ass? That beast is down there killing friends and foes alike. Gryton and I were trying to toast her when we saw what was happening up here." The Null was panting and had to pause for a moment to catch her breath. "Is there anything else we can do to help here?"

"Not here, no," Thayn said. "But if you don't destroy the blood witch and her evil work, there may be nothing for the Avatars to return to if we don't finish this."

"I'm not sure if we can reach the witch. Every time we try, her power does something that disturbs the dragon's fire magic. It's like what the djinn tried with his assassin spell, but this is different, and he hasn't found a way to counteract it yet. And I've hit my upper limit and can't neutralize her power."

"Gryton and Erika, if there were another option, I wouldn't ask this of you. But you have to do whatever you must to keep the blood witch's spells from reaching the rift in the Veil." Thayn looked at Anna and the others. "The rest of us will protect Lillian."

"I will not fail," the dragon roared, nearly deafening everyone.

Erika merely held her arms wide. "Drink up. I need to make room to absorb more magic, but I can't stay long. Got a witch to kill."

Anna and her Rasoren didn't take the Null up on her offer, not trusting what would happen if they absorbed any more magic into their already stressed bodies. But the others approached and accepted the gift she offered.

Once they and the legion gargoyles had fed upon the Null's purified magic, Erika ran back to her dragon mount and strapped herself back into her harness.

"Give the witch a beating for me!" Anna shouted.

The Null's laughter reached her a moment later, and then the girl and her dragon were gone, plummeting down the side of a mountain at breakneck speed. The dragon breathed fire on any enemy in his path.

"Thanks, Gryton," Anna whispered. "You're not so bad after all. Don't get killed and bring Erika back safely too."

CHAPTER THIRTY-THREE

Gryton

While they'd been with Anna and the others, the blood witch's spell had been busy and had spread to cover three times the area it had covered before. What was left of the demigoddess's temple was now completely covered in thick ropes of power and blood. They twisted and scrambled down the stairway and reached across the valley floor, covering everything it encountered like a bindweed trying to outgrow all the competition.

"Damn. That fuck-nasty is spreading fast. Any idea how we kill it?"

"I'm still studying it," he rumbled in reply.

He darted closer and breathed fire upon the nearest section of vines. The portions his flame touched turned to ash, and the rest withered and churned like the fire caused them pain.

He struck repeatedly, diving and flaming. After the tenth such attack, the plant's behavior changed, and it sent tendrils after him. Where it touched, his flames leaped up wildly, and Gryton hastily darted out of range.

"That's another type of assassin spell. Stay the hell away from that shit," she barked.

"I would if I could, but the vine is beginning to climb itself like it's growing its own tower. If it's left unchecked, it will reach the rift in the sky."

"Damn it."

"Indeed," he agreed. "There is so much of it, I could burn away portions of it for the next thousand years and might never get it all. We need to find the source and destroy it."

"Sounds good. How the hell do we find the source?"

"I'm certain the source is the blood witch's soul."

He felt the Null's hesitation, but at last she asked, "The witch's soul will be buried deep in that vine. The attempt will kill you, won't it?"

"I already know where her soul is." He paused before telling her the rest. "And, yes, I will lose mastery over my form, but my soul will live on in the heavens."

"Then I'm proud to fight and die at your side, Gryton."

"And I would be honored to die by your side," he said in return, then looked ahead. "But I have no plans on allowing you to die with me."

He slashed the harness holding her in place, and then as she started to slide to one side, he caught her and gently cradled her in one of his front claws.

"What are you doing?"

"Destroying the witch and saving you, my Null."

"No! I'll fight to the end at your side."

"Not this time."

He might know defeat this day, but he would make his mother proud and still protect his Null at the same time. He slowed enough to gently deposit her on the ground. Then he rose higher into the sky, screaming challenges at the threat. But this enemy would fall like the others of her kind before her. The powers of the lightless void were no match for the purifying fire of an elemental dragon.

He raced toward the witch, no longer trying to avoid her traps and strikes. He just blew right through them until he, at last, reached the core of her power, the twisted darkness that had once been her soul.

Exhaling a deep breath, his fire raced across the distance and burned away the taint holding the great spell together.

It came at a cost, though. Even as the witch's spell disintegrated around him, so did his own mastery of his fire magic. The witch would have her own revenge upon him, but that didn't matter. He'd fulfilled his purpose and Erika was safe.

As if thinking of the Null summoned her, she was suddenly in his mind again.

"Dragon. What have you done?"

"Destroyed the witch."

"I know." She paused, and he felt her sob. "But what about you?"

"I shall die now and be reborn a sun."

Erika couldn't stop the sobs that shook her body. He was dying. She'd known there was only a slim chance that they'd survive, but she thought they'd die together.

"Not this time." The dragon's voice was gentle, and she realized that in the moment of their death, both Gryton and his dragon nature had finally stopped fighting. "You are my one true friend. Keep me in your heart. Remember me, because everyone should have at least one loved one who will live to keep their memory alive."

He hovered in the air, no longer needing to beat his wings.

"Tell my mother I loved her when next you see her."

"I will."

Then he rose higher, his flames expanding to twice the size they'd been before.

"Goodbye. I'm sorry I wasn't kinder to you, and I hope this last act has made me worthy."

"You are worthy, Gryton. Lillian and Gregory will be so very proud of you. And I will miss you, my friend."

But then he was streaking away, a vaguely dragon-shaped radiant ball of energy racing out to space, trailing fire. He looked like a comet. More tears gathered in her eyes until her vision blurred, but she continued to watch until he was just another star against the black sky.

"I'll see you again one day, in this life or the next. Goodbye, my Dragon."

CHAPTER THIRTY-FOUR

Anna

They could only watch as the dragon sacrificed himself, but he'd succeeded in destroying the witch before her spell could reach the rift in the veil. While the dragon and the Null had been busy battling the witch, Anna and Obsidian and their beleaguered allies, had been fighting for their lives, too.

But the enemy soldiers never reached Lillian.

"We've won." Obsidian's exhausted whisper barely reached her sensitive ears.

She turned to him and saw that his wings were drooping, and his skin was more grayish than its usual lustrous black.

"You need to find a safe place to rest before you embrace the stone sleep."

"Soon." He stumbled away from her, and it wasn't until she darted around his wings that she saw where he was headed.

She stopped short, not wanting to intrude on the pooka's grief, but also wanting to support him if he wanted a shoulder to cry on. The pooka had shed his black pony form for that of a black-haired, yellow-eyed youth.

He was hunched over the dead body of the unicorn, sobbing while Gran held him with an arm around his shoulders. "Shhh. The unicorn knows that you loved him like a brother."

"I was terrible to him," the pooka said in a broken voice, "but he was always my friend."

"I am sorry," Obsidian said and patted the pooka gently. "He fought bravely. He saved my life."

Anna hadn't even realized how close she'd come to losing Obsidian, but she saw in his mind how the unicorn had lunged and taken out an enemy soldier before the woman could release her arrow into Obsidian's heart.

God. She'd come so close to losing him.

Anna knelt in the churned-up mud and blood and rested a hand on the unicorn's neck. "Thank you, my friend. Until we meet again in the Spirit Realm."

She stood then and followed Obsidian to his next destination. He led her to the cliff. Midway down the slope River's body rested propped against Darkness. A healer was with the pair, but after Anna and Obsidian scrambled down the slope, she saw as the healer gave that ever so slight shake of head that said the person was beyond the ability to heal.

Anna had seen that too many times in the last two days.

Obsidian crouched next to his mother, weeping along with his father.

River's pale skin was already a grayish tone, and her body was covered in bright blood.

"Did we win?" she asked Stalks the Darkness in what was probably supposed to be a private link, but she didn't have the strength to shield it.

"Yes, my love," Darkness said as he gathered her in his arms and tried to get her to drink some of his blood, but Anna already knew no amount of gargoyle blood could save her.

"I love you and our children. I should have told you that more often. I couldn't have asked for a better family. I'm proud to be Lillian and Obsidian's mother."

The dryad fell silent then, and Anna thought she'd lost consciousness, but then her voice continued in their thoughts.

"Darkness, I hope you find love again one day. A true love. A female worthy of you as I never was. I'm sorry for my part in keeping you a prisoner for all those years."

"It is already forgiven. And you are my true mate, and I love you. One day I'll see you in the Spirit Realm."

River's eyes never opened again. A short time later, she exhaled one last time, her chest stilling.

Obsidian cried, rocking himself softly.

Anna went to him then and wrapped her arms and wings around him. "I'm here. I won't leave you. Sleep now."

When he stopped rocking, she realized it was because he'd surrendered to the stone sleep.

"Darkness, I have no right to ask this of you, but will you see that your son and I are protected. I fear we can no longer protect ourselves."

She saw the other male snatch at her request like it was a lifeline. And perhaps it was. Gargoyles were protectors, and now he had something to protect again. "Of course, Kyrsu. Rest peacefully knowing you and my son are safe."

"Thank you."

Sighing, Anna cuddled closer to Obsidian and rested her head on his shoulder as she wrapped her tail around him.

"Sleep well, my love," she whispered before she, too, gave in to the call of the stone sleep.

CHAPTER THIRTY-FIVE

Lillian

Waking was more difficult than usual, and Lillian instantly knew something was very, very wrong even before she opened her eyes. There was a hollowness inside her. It was familiar. She'd felt it before. Her soul was gone like the time it had lived in her hamadryad. But this time it was much worse. She couldn't feel Gregory. Couldn't sense him.

Gregory?

When she opened her eyes, she discovered she was in a tent. A swift glance around showed she was alone except for a stone statue with Gregory's likeness. He sat off in the shadows at the other end of the tent.

She stumbled to her feet. Wobbling unsteadily, she made it to his side.

"Gregory?" She called to him again, but he didn't answer nor did his skin warm under her hand.

"He's gone," Thayn said as he appeared in the tent beside her. "I'm sorry. I know the pain of losing a loved one."

Then he took her in his arms and comforted her, holding her while she sobbed. When she quieted, he told her everything that had happened.

It was hard to speak, but she forced words out. "The Sorceress ensured I would live so I can raise Gregory's child?"

"Yes. She couldn't face the thought of losing the child." He paused and then continued. "But there is a cost for existing without your soul or the magic of the Avatars. You will not live much beyond ten years."

"Just long enough to see my gargoyle daughter born," she breathed. "But my child will live?"

"Yes. And I swear upon my soul I will help Vivien raise the girlchild into a woman to make her Avatar parents very proud."

A sense of devastation overtook her for a few minutes, and yet she understood why the Sorceress ensured that Lillian lived. She wanted to give her daughter a chance at life.

The old gargoyle cleared his throat. "But if you're up for one more adventure, you might have a chance at the life you and Gregory wanted—that big family with lots of little ones."

His words breathed new hope into her charred and hollowed out heart. If there was any way to get Gregory back and restore herself to the Sorceress...

Then Thayn laid out his plan with all the risks and the rewards. But if she was successful at reaching the Avatar in the Spirit Realm and could convince it to sever its soul in two once more, she might have the life she and Gregory always wanted.

Darkness joined them then, walking in through the open tent flap with Gran only a few steps behind him.

Vivien ran to her and gave Lillian a fierce hug. "My darling. Thank the Mother Goddess. Thayn said you'd wake. And I knew you would. You're such a fighter. But knowing something and seeing it with my own eyes isn't at all the same."

Gran gave her two more hugs before she stepped back to allow Darkness his turn. It was after her father finally released her that Lillian learned about her mother's death. That came as a surprising blow, and she wasn't at all sure how to process that news. She'd only known her mother a short time, and they hadn't necessarily gotten along as well as they could have, but the news that she would never see her birth mother again brought fresh tears to her eyes.

Then she learned that Jason and Greenborrow were both still missing.

"I know they are alive," Gran said with passion. "I'd know it if either of them was dead. We just haven't found them yet is all. They're probably out chasing escaped enemies."

Lillian could only hope that was true. And while she wanted to join the hunt for them, she also knew if they'd been captured, the Avatars would be able to find them much swifter than any search party.

She said as much aloud and demanded to know more about what she'd have to do to win back her soul.

"It won't be an easy task, my daughter," Darkness cautioned. "The Avatar always prefers to be one and only separates at the Divine Ones' command. This time there is no danger to the three realms to move the Divine Ones into giving such an order."

She sucked in a breath. "I understand."

"The Avatar may not wish to experience the pain of separation again so soon, even if such a thing is possible," Darkness continued to explain. "And the soul might be too weakened for what you ask even if the Avatar is willing. But if you wish to go, I will carry you to the Spirit Realm since that is within my power to do."

It was a risk. A great one and the outcome uncertain. But if she didn't go, she would always regret not trying.

"How soon can we go?"

CHAPTER THIRTY-SIX

Lillian

The realm of spirits was nothing like what Lillian envisioned. She looked out over a long, flat prairie. A silvery magic floated around her like mist. Her father had explained that this was a transition place, not the true afterlife and that the mist could be used to shape anything the heart desired.

He'd taken her as far as his own bodily limits had allowed. Unlike her, his body wasn't designed to house the soul of an Avatar. As a result, he couldn't travel as far as her into the Spirit Realm. But before she'd left him to continue on, he'd cautioned her not to shape the mist into anything.

It would be far too easy to conjure up Gregory and live here until her body gave out from lack of food and water. Then she'd die without ever reaching the Avatar. Her father had also told her as host to the soul, she would be able to sense the Avatar and track it.

Though likely the Avatar would sense her long before she found it.

That was what Lillian was hoping for when a white equine shape came galloping out of the mist. At first, she thought her subconscious mind had summoned the unicorn. But then as he pranced his way closer, she doubted she would summon anything so silly acting.

"Hello, my friend," she called to him.

"Lillian, I came as soon as I heard you had arrived. I knew you were a brave one." He lowered his head for a scratch just like he had when he'd been alive.

"Are you okay?" she asked him.

"As good as new. Better actually. Though, I miss my friends back on the mortal world. And I don't know what that dour pooka will do without me." He bobbed his head and nuzzled her. "But enough talk of me. Would you like a ride to your Avatar?"

"Please!"

The stallion nickered in humor and then presented his side for her to mount. She didn't have to be asked twice. Then they were galloping toward her future.

When she finally looked upon the Avatar—ethereal silvery-blue power floating from its elegant body like mist rising off the ocean—she was humbled by the being's beauty and strength. Graceful wings trailed behind the being like a cloak, and from the shimmering mists, a long, powerful tail appeared, its tip flicking in a familiar manner as it swirled the surrounding mist-like power slowly.

Even over the distance, she could feel the immense flows of magic the Avatar commanded burning along her skin. As she watched in absolute silence, barely daring to breathe for fear she would distract the Avatar at a critical moment, the spirit being injected a substantial flow of magic into a section of the Veil Between the Realms.

Strengthening it? Repairing it?

After a time, the Avatar shifted, moving to a new section of the Veil, closer to Lillian's location. Nearer now, she had a better view and could more easily study the spirit's beauty. Its surprisingly human—or sidhe-like—face now in profile, she noted the hard line of a jaw contrasting with the softer curve of a cheek. A hint of full lips. A broad brow. The more she studied it, the more androgynous it appeared.

But one thing was certain, its features held an otherworldly beauty that stole her breath.

The sublime being was a strange mix of the Gargoyle Protector and his Sorceress. The two halves of the soul truly were one being. It was one thing to be told but something else entirely to see it. This was the true Avatar of the Divine Ones. One being made whole at last.

What right did she have to ask for such a great sacrifice? To ask for it to split itself in two just so one mortal gargoyle-dryad hybrid could live out a dream that was never meant to be?

A sob built in her throat. She closed her fist in the unicorn's mane.

"Let's go. I don't belong here. I've intruded enough."

"You want to go now? But we only just arrived, and the Avatar will want to see you before you return to the Magic Realm."

"I can't face the Avatar. I never should have come. And I certainly have no right to ask it to make such a sacrifice for me." Tears rolled down her cheeks. "Please go."

"My Lillian, do not go so soon."

That beautiful voice sent a chill down her spine. She looked up toward the sound, craving to hear more. And she recognized something of her beloved gargoyle in its rich tones.

The mists swirled around the titan's legs as the Avatar moved toward her; its strides too graceful to be called anything other than a slow prowl. Lillian took a dozen steps back before she could stop herself. The being didn't react to her show of fear, merely kneeling gracefully before her.

Had there been sun or shadow in this place, she would have been shrouded in darkness, dwarfed by the titan's immense size.

Her heart, already pounding in her chest, beat harder as the Avatar reached out and touched her, caressing one finger along her entire right side.

"It has only been a short time, but I have already missed you, my Lillian."

Strangely, the Avatar sounded more male by the moment. As she watched, she saw a gradual shift in the spirit creature's appearance and suddenly it didn't just sound more like a 'he,' it looked it as well. One specific male. Her gargoyle.

And then that powerful mind reached out and touched

her thoughts with the kindness she'd come to expect of her beloved mate.

"Gregory?"

"Yes. I was known as Gregory. Your mate." The creature frowned, his mobile ears emerging from his thick mane and flicked hesitantly, as if he was deep in thought. "It is strange to think of myself as male in this place. I am not male or female here and yet somehow your presence has triggered a change in me. I wonder why that is?" He paused again and a gentle smile played across his lips. "Come, my love. Let me hold you."

She reached for him eagerly, climbing on the titan's large hand, then uncaring if she appeared foolish or weak or weepy, she clung to one of his fingers.

He held her in that gentle cage of spirit and shimmering power for what might have been hours as she poured out her grief at losing him.

Eventually, she finished sobbing, her tears drying.

"I came here because I wanted you back," she said at last. "I wanted the Gargoyle Protector and the Mother's Sorceress to be able to have the family you've always wanted. I wanted you to see your daughter born, to teach her and guide her. And then I wanted the same for Gryton if he still lives."

The Avatar laughed, his grin stunning. "That one is far harder to kill than anyone knows. Our son still lives and will return to us one day."

"I am glad." A fresh flood of tears spilled down her face. "Damn it. I can't stop crying."

"Do not worry," he crooned softly. "Tears are never a weakness. But you say you came here because you wanted me back and yet now you sound as if you've changed your mind."

"Because seeing you as you truly are, seeing you complete like this, made me realize how selfish I was to want you to sacrifice so much just to return to me. You have sacrificed enough. You deserve to be happy here where you belong."

"I remember what it was like to love you. I would return to the living for you even without the promise of children and a family." He grinned again. "Though, of course, I want a family if you are willing. You are offering me, offering us, the one thing we have always wanted."

"You want to return with me?" She stood straighter as eagerness and hope pumped through her blood.

"Yes. More than anything. But it is not without great risk. You will have to carry both halves of the Avatar soul back to the Magic Realm. And once there, you will need to convince the male half to release you and return to his own body."

"Thayn told me as much."

"Yes, but that is the greatest hardship for the Avatars. And I'm not sure if my male half will be strong enough to do what he must. Lillian, you may need to be strong enough for us both and convince him to give up the most perfect of bonds for another type of bond that is less perfect but has the chance to be even more rewarding. Are you willing to risk this? If you fail, I will remain with you until your life is over." The Avatar paused as if remembering something. "Hosting both halves of the Avatar soul will bring you a swifter death. Your body isn't designed to carry both halves of my soul."

"For a lifetime together, to live in peace and raise our children, I would risk far more." She paused as something else occurred to her. "What about our daughter. If I die before she is born, will it bring about her death as well?"

"Normally it would, but I can share enough magic with the hamadryad tree to last many, many years. That way, even if we fail, our daughter will live on."

Grinning as a weight lifted off her chest, she held her arms out wide. "I eagerly accept you into my body."

The Avatar shimmered, losing form and then he came to her, entering her body with a great gentleness and care, as if he was making love to her.

All that shimmering power flooded into her, sinking into her skin and pumping through her blood where it finally came to rest just below her heart. It was the most glorious feeling, as if he touched her everywhere, filling up every lonely corner of her mind. It was divinely perfect. Then it was over. She was now full, brimming with power and knowledge.

For the first time since waking in the tent, she felt complete.

But the Avatar soon guided her back the way she'd come. There was a rushed urgency to the journey this time. Fleetingly, the memory of the Avatar's warning, of how her body couldn't contain both halves of the soul for long, surfaced and she understood the reason for the rush.

Slowly Lillian's surroundings faded. She surrendered to the Avatar, trusting the spirit creature to know what to do.

CHAPTER THIRTY-SEVEN

Lillian

She awoke with the sense she'd slept a few hours, though her body was still exhausted. The sun was rising, a new day beginning as she opened her eyes and looked around. The walls of a tent again met her gaze.

Both the tent and her lack of magic were familiar. There was something else too. She still lacked a soul.

The Avatar in the Spirit Realm—was it all a dream?

Please, no. Not a dream.

"It was real. This is real," said a most familiar and beloved voice.

A moment later strong arms encircled her and pulled her out of the cot where she'd been sleeping.

"There was no way we would both fit on that tiny bed,

so I took the floor. However, I think I'd prefer to be your bed." Gregory nuzzled her and then started giving her sloppy gargoyle kisses before settling her on his chest.

"Gregory! You're here!"

"Yes." His happy rumble was accompanied by a few more licks. "And you are the bravest, most determined mate in all the realms. I don't deserve you."

She snorted. "You're going to get exactly what you deserve; a very long vacation and then a future filled with many children, grandchildren, and great-grandchildren. Is there anything else you'd like before I accept your surrender?"

"No." Purring, he ran his hands along her sides. "Do you wish to get started now?"

Grinning, she turned her head and pressed a kiss to his cheek. "As tempting as that is, I think I need a bath first and then maybe a bigger bed. Though I'd like to know one thing."

"Yes, my love?"

"Where's my half of the Avatar soul? Not that I'm complaining. But I seem to have misplaced her."

"We discussed that while I was still the Avatar. I put you in the hamadryad here in the Magic Realm and then migrated into the tree. From there, the hamadryad sent the male half of my soul back into this body, and the female half stayed in the hamadryad. Does that arrangement still please you?"

"It's perfect. Any arrangement is fine with me."

"I have something else to ask."

"Anything."

"If you are not averse to the idea, I'd like to stay here and claim a conqueror's rights and remake the Battle Goddess's kingdom into the new home for Second Legion."

"Of course." Lillian didn't really care where she lived as long as her loved ones were with her or came to visit. And seeing how Gran and Thayn's 'friendship' was developing, she imagined Gran would find excuses to visit the Magic Realm a great deal.

"Good, because the hamadryad Sorceress has already moved your hamadryad from Earth to the grove here to have our child as close as possible. She also brought all the little potted hamadryads you were growing. I think she's impatient to expand on our little family."

Lillian braced on her elbows so she could stare down into his eyes. "I take it our daughter and my tree are both fine?"

"Yes. Very. Greenborrow and Jason are already mapping out a new maze to plant around the trees."

"Jason's alive? Greenborrow survived, too? Gran and the others had lost track of them in the fighting, and no one had found him by the time I went to the Spirit Realm."

"They were busy hunting down an incubus-hybrid who had killed Whitethorn."

"Thayn told me about Whitethorn's death. The Leader of the Hunt will be remembered."

"He fought bravely. Everyone fought bravely; although, all factions of our alliance lost a lot of good people. You'll be pleased to know Major Resnick survived, as did the rest of his unit. They were either lucky, blessed by the Divine Ones, or humans are a lot more formidable than I'd originally judged. Though they took some substantial injuries. But the healers have seen to them and say all of Resnick's team will live."

Lillian's heart lightened a little more with each piece of good news.

Gregory suddenly cupped her cheek. "I had Anna and Obsidian moved to the new grove. They will recover and wake in a year or two. They just need rest and time to adjust to their new powers. As for Darkness, he has spent his time watching over them and you," Gregory paused again and gave her a gentle squeeze, "and holding vigil over your mother's body."

"I should go to my father. Be there with him."

"He would rather you rest and grow strong once more. He'll perform the returning to nature ritual in two days. Many other such ceremonies will be held at the same time. We wished to give the other magic wielders time to heal or travel here so they can grieve together before the rituals of mourning.

"That is wise." She swallowed hard. "Do we know how many we lost?"

"We are still trying to determine that. We are also trying to determine how many of the enemy escaped to Earth through the portal spell."

"Goddess. The military back home wasn't able to contain them?"

"They weren't given a chance. Naharnin shifted the portal's exit point. They arrived on Earth north of the original anchor."

"We have to do something." Lillian started to rise. "Naharnin is too dangerous to leave on Earth."

"I know. The Sorceress hamadryad already has a plan in the works."

CHAPTER THIRTY-EIGHT

Gregory

There was no stopping Lillian once she'd made up her mind and soon Gregory found himself escorting his beloved mate to her two hamadryad trees to check that all was well. Not that she didn't trust him, but she said it was a mother's right to worry all the same.

He'd waited for Lillian to satisfy herself about the health of their child before he approached the subject of Naharnin again.

"The Sorceress and I are both concerned about Naharnin being on Earth. It could be disastrous."

"I feel fine. We should go at once and find him. I may not have my powers of the Sorceress at the moment, but I have all my memories. I know how dangerous a trapped djinn is."

"Yes. But you cannot go."

"Why?" Her eyes narrowed. "You're not about to go all over-the-top protective on me, are you?"

"That is a distinct possibility, but that is not why we can't go." His hands, which had been resting on her shoulders, moved down her arms and then came to rest on her hips for a moment before his thumbs caressed her belly.

"There was another complication the Avatar did not foresee."

Her eyes widened, and then she glanced down at her flat belly. "Do you mean a baby? But how?"

Gregory coughed, and he knew a sheepish look was covering his face. "The Avatar is a source of the Divine Ones' creative power."

"Keep talking."

"The Avatar was feeling uncharacteristically male when his mortal mate journeyed all the way to the Spirit Realm to find him. It wasn't planned or intentional, but the creative energies sparked."

She leaned back, her eyes going wide again. "Are we going to have another Gryton?"

"No. This child won't be like either Gryton or our gargoyle daughter. This one will be more like a djinn. That is why we can't return to the Mortal Realm. The child can't survive in that magicless place until he or she is much older." He paused, uncertain if she blamed him. "Are you angry at the Avatar?"

"No. I'm not angry." She smiled gently. "Though I'm going to point out that you're talking about yourself in the third person."

"Both halves of the Avatar soul were together then, so in a sense I differ from that being." He shrugged.

"I'm just joking with you." She stood on her tiptoes to kiss him.

A wave of giddiness bled off her, and she chuckled until tears ran down her face.

"And what is so humorous, my Lady?"

"Are we ever going to have a 'planned' pregnancy?"

His lips twisted in humor. "That would be Gryton. We planned for him."

He watched as her humor died as swiftly as it had come. "He'll come back, won't he?"

"Of course he will. He loves you. And the Null; he loves her, too. Though I think the dragon is the only one who has figured that out."

Lillian snorted. "Gryton's delightfully oblivious to the fact, isn't he?"

"Yes."

After a time, Lillian came to stand between the three hamadryads and looked upon her oldest tree where it grew near her mother's. "You said the Sorceress was working on the Naharnin issue. In what way? Because if we can't go after him and Anna and Obsidian will sleep for a year or more, and who knows how long before Gryton's return, how will we find and free Naharnin?"

"You may not like it." Gregory wasn't sure how he felt about it himself. It would mean his other half returning to the Mortal Realm without him since he couldn't leave Lillian while she was pregnant with their djinn child. She would need his magic to keep her and the baby strong. "But the Sorceress has cloned your body." He held up his hand to forestall the many questions he saw in her gaze. "Be at ease. The Sorceress knows she has time to grow the body properly this time. It will be safe. It won't be Daryna all over again. I can promise you that."

He could see it as his mate worked through the emotional impact of the news he'd just shared. At last, she sighed, leaned in close, and pressed another kiss to his jaw.

"Do not worry my gargoyle. I can't very well get bent out of shape since this was the Sorceress's plan—my plan—since I first discovered how Naharnin viewed us. I wished to correct the mistake of how we treated him. So, if either of us should ask forgiveness, it is I who should ask for your forgiveness. Though, I wouldn't have created a second me without your permission. But apparently hamadryad me doesn't worry about niceties like that."

Once again, his mate had managed to surprise him. He doubted she'd ever lose the ability. "You are okay with the hamadryad's actions?"

"Yes. I'm okay with just about anything as long as we're together." Lillian reached down and captured his hand, giving it a tug. "Come on. I see Greenborrow headed this way. I want to talk about designing the new maze. And if we're going to be stuck in the Magic Realm for a while, I know some hamadryad cuttings that would likely be happier in the ground."

Lillian looked at the area, studying the three trees. Her expression turned sad when her gaze settled on her mother's tree. "Do you think the Sorceress can keep my mother's tree alive as a monument to her bravery and sacrifice? It would also give my father a place to mourn."

"Your hamadryad is you. She has likely already read

your secret wishes and seen that they are done, but if you wish to be certain, simply communicate with her. That is always within your power. After all, you and your hamadryad are one being. Thus, you are still and will always be my Sorceress."

"And you are my beloved Gargoyle Protector always. No matter what lives we live."

EPILOGUE

Erika

This was her last night in the Magic Realm, Erika reflected as she stared up at the night sky. She'd be returning to Earth shortly with the last team. Gregory had secured permission for her to stay this long, saying he wanted to make certain she hadn't sustained damage from the battle or the dragon's abrupt and violent transformation into a star.

But Erika secretly thought the gargoyle demigod was allowing her the time she needed to deal with her grief over the loss of her dragon. He'd thought she needed these last few nights. And he'd been correct. Coming here and sitting on this bench next to the hamadryads and gazing up at the sky, watching as stars spun by, did help. Though there was only one she was interested in.

Tonight, the sky was darker, the stars easier to see since none of the three moons had yet risen. She was so focused on the sky, she almost missed the stirring in the darkness to the right of the bench, but her ability awoke a moment before the shadows shivered and Gregory appeared beside her.

She nodded in welcome as he settled on the bench next to her. The Avatar looked up at the sky for a moment before his deep voice reached out to her. "What is my son up to this night?"

"Much the same as usual, I assume."

Some secret amusement twinkled in his eyes while he regarded her, but at last he told her what was on his mind. "You are uniquely able to track his recovery if you so wish."

Erika sat up straighter. "What are you talking about."

"Your soul-link with my son." He tipped his head to indicate her chest.

Reaching up, she placed her hand over her breast. Then, as if acknowledging her, a small tendril of magic expanded out from the soul-shard and flared along her mind.

There were no words, but she felt a growing warmth, and then emotions too wild and chaotic to decipher flooded into her mind.

"Do you feel my son?"

"Yes." She glanced up at him. "Why didn't you tell me about this before? I've been worried about him."

"I know. But it wasn't a lie when I said I needed to ensure you hadn't been harmed by the dragon's transformation. I've only now determined you've recovered enough from all the battle magic you absorbed that it is safe for you to attempt to touch the dragon."

The gargoyle looked up at the night sky. A smile touched his lips. "You will be good for my son. But don't get yourself killed while the dragon is indisposed. It will anger him a great deal. He'd probably storm the Spirit Realm to get you back. I'd prefer a dragon not go rampaging through my home while I'm away."

Erika snorted. "I'll try not to get killed then."

"Good."

"But what happens if I die of old age before he returns?"

"I suppose we'll have to deal with that if it happens." The gargoyle didn't sound too concerned by the possibility. "I shall leave you to your thoughts. Goodbye Private Erika Emerson, oldest of the First Wave and greatest of the Nulls. Our paths will cross again one day."

Then the gargoyle summoned the shadows and vanished as swiftly as he'd come.

"Wait!" Erika jumped off the bench. "And... you're gone."

The Avatar might have left her with more questions than she'd started with, but he'd also told her she could still sense and track Gryton's progress. That was a great gift she hadn't even known she still possessed.

She pressed her palm against her chest again. As had happened before, the soul-link flared with warmth.

A foolish wave of happy tears flowed down her cheeks.

"Are those tears for me? I'm going to start to think you care, Null," whispered a voice that was equal parts haughty, familiar, and beloved. *"We'll see each other again one day."*

"Gryton! We *will* see each other again! I'll accept nothing less from you!" More tears flowed down her cheeks.

Some part of Gryton still lived inside that star, and she would have faith her friend would return. She felt another flicker of his mirth, but he didn't speak again, and soon even that spark of personality was lost under the chaotic churn of a feral fire elemental's ravenous desires.

But she'd felt him in her mind, and the piece of his soul she kept safe was still a warmth in her chest. He'd return to her one day. She knew in her heart that he would.

"Ho there!" Another, gruffer voice called out to her.

She turned toward the sound and saw Greenborrow in the company of the pooka and the banshee approaching her. "Private Emerson. We'll be returning to the Mortal Realm shortly to help with the hunt for the Battle Goddess's underlings on Earth. Gregory said he saw you here. Thought you'd like to come with us. You ready to leave?"

"I am now." She started to follow them but paused and glanced up at her dragon star one last time. "But I have a feeling the Magic Realm isn't done with me yet."

THE END

Lillian and Gregory's tale may have come to an end, but Corporal Anna Mackenzie and Obsidian's adventures will continue in Legacy of Shadows coming in 2022. And then

Private Erika Emerson and her grumpy elemental dragon later in 2023.

Hey before you go, can I interest you in signing up for my author newsletter? You get my free starter library as a gift for joining.

http://lisablackwood.com/join-the-newsletter-here/

Did you enjoy Sorceress Eternal? If you have a moment and wouldn't mind leaving a review, that would be greatly appreciated. Reviews help other readers to decide if a book is something they would like. It doesn't need to be long. Even a few words can be tremendously helpful.

None of this would have been possible without, you, my readers. You're awesome! Thank You!

Bye for now,
Lisa Blackwood

ABOUT THE AUTHOR

Lisa Blackwood is the author of the bestselling Gargoyle and Sorceress urban fantasy series. Her work has also landed on the Wall Street Journal and the USA Today Bestseller lists as part of the Dominion Rising Anthology. When she's not reading and writing, she also enjoys gardening and spending time with her horse and her dogs.

At present, she grudgingly lives in a small town in Southern Ontario, though she would much rather live deep in a dark forest, surrounded by majestic old-growth trees. Since she cannot live her fantasy, she decided to write fantasy instead.

BOOKS BY LISA BLACKWOOD

Gargoyle & Sorceress

Dawn of the Sorceress

Sorceress Awakening

Sorceress Rising

Sorceress Hunting

Sorceress at War

Sorceress Enraged

Legacy of the Sorceress

Sorcery & Firedrakes

Scion of the Sorceress

Sorceress Eternal

In Deception's Shadow Series (Epic Fantasy Romance)

Betrayal's Price

Herd Mistress

Maiden's Wolf

Death's Queen

The Prince's Gryphon (forthcoming)

Ishtar's Legacy Series (Epic Fantasy Romance)

Ishtar's Blade

The Blade's Beginning (short story)

Blade's Honor

Blade's Destiny

The Blade's Shadow

First Queen of the Gryphons

The King of the Anunnaki (forthcoming)

The Anunnaki's Blade (forthcoming)

Huntress vs Huntsman (Epic Fantasy Romance)

Master of the Hunt

Night Huntress

Dragon Archer

Soul Mage (forthcoming)